Up North Murder

CT

Cheryl Taylor

An Up North Michigan Mystery

FIRST EDITION October 2016

Cover Design by Cheryl Taylor
Cover Photograph by Cheryl Taylor

ISBN: 978-0-9982122-0-3

Printed in the United States

Published by:
CT Communications
9535 E. Marilyn Ln.
Dewey, AZ 86327
cfaytay@gmail.com
cherylftaylor.com

Edited by: Linda Schwandt
Schwandt Editorial Services

To
Greg
My Motivation and Inspiration
Thank you

Books by Cheryl Taylor

Gone to Ground

Up North Michigan Cozy Mystery Series
Up North Murder (Book One)

The full moon was peeking over the pines on the opposite side of the lake, leaving a trail of liquid silver across the water leading up to Gordon Dorsey's dock. Up on the first floor deck of his cedar and field stone house, Gordon leaned back in his chair and sipped his beer. He closed his eyes in enjoyment, savoring the nutty, fruity flavor. This was the result of his first experiment in brewing cherry beer and he felt pleased with the effort. Definitely worth repeating in his opinion.

He relaxed back into his Adirondack chair, eyes closed. A gentle breeze stirred the pines, the resulting murmur rising and falling. The loons swimming on the lake called back and forth, their haunting voices lulled Gordon toward sleep. The frogs and crickets added their voices to the music of the forest.

At his feet, Max, Gordon's small, female Australian Shepherd raised her head. Nose in the air she sniffed, then got to her feet and quietly disappeared around the corner of the house at a trot. A short time later he heard a bark in the distance. Minutes passed, and Gordon debated between checking on Max, and staying on the deck. *Probably a raccoon after the fish. Max will take care of it,* he thought, and settled back into the chair.

Gradually Gordon became aware of the low hum of a vehicle approaching from the west, tires crunching on the gravel of his long, two-rut driveway. *Busy night,* he thought. Unwilling to let go of the peaceful evening and sure that regardless of who the driver was, at this time of night it had to be a friend, he remained in his chair, eyes closed. He heard the engine sputter to a stop, a door opened then slammed shut, and the sound of footsteps on pea gravel leading up to the back porch. A quick knock on the back door followed.

"Round front," Gordon called back, still not bothering to open his eyes.

He heard the footsteps retreat off the back porch, then silence as the visitor presumably traversed the dirt path along the side of the house toward the front, the pine duff absorbing all sound. He opened his eyes and sat up as he heard his evening guest began to mount the stairs leading to the front deck. A figure emerged from the shadows at the corner of the house, moving into the soft radiance shed by the moon.

"Hello, Gordon. I guess we need to have a talk." The visitor walked over to a second chair near Gordon's and sat down.

"I guess we do, at that," replied Gordon, as he relaxed back into his seat. "You want some cherry beer?"

"Abby? Abby! Abby, are you okay? What's going on?"

The voice gradually penetrated through the fog in Abigail Williams' brain, pulling her back to the real world.

She looked up and saw Lucy Atkins, colleague and close friend, standing in the doorway, a concerned look on her face.

"Oh. Hey, Luce, come on in."

The petite brunette stepped farther into the room. "You were worlds away," Lucy remarked, studying Abby's face carefully. "Something going on? Your favorite restaurant close? You miss a great shoe sale? Your goldfish die?" Lucy smiled as she came and sat in the chair on the far side of Abby's desk.

"No, not my goldfish. My uncle."

"Oh, God, Abby. I'm so sorry!" Lucy leaned forward over the large maple desk, reaching her hand out toward her friend. "Me and my big mouth. What happened?"

Abby took Lucy's hand and gave it a quick squeeze, then let go and sat up straighter in the large brown leather desk chair which sat with its back to the large wall of windows. She glanced down briefly at the phone sitting on the blotter in front of her as though it held all the answers but wasn't spilling the details.

"I'm not really sure. It's strange. I just got a call from a lawyer, some guy named Rick Laskis, telling me that my

Uncle Gordon has died. He said I was named as executor of his estate, but he didn't seem to want to give me any details over the phone."

Abby chewed thoughtfully on her lower lip as a small frown line appeared between her hazel eyes. She looked back up at Lucy, meeting her friend's concerned gaze. "He wants me to come up there to go over the details."

"Where exactly is 'up there'?"

"Well, my uncle lived on a farm somewhere near a small town called Millersburg in northern Michigan. This lawyer, though, he was in what passes for a large city in those parts, a place called Alpena."

"Were you and your uncle close?" Lucy asked. "I mean, you've never mentioned him."

"No, not really." Abby shook her head slightly, her shoulder length, light brown hair swinging gently. "I haven't seen him in years. Not since I was a teenager." Her eyes took on a distant look as she remembered the past.

"He was quite a bit older than my mother, his sister. My mother said he made the Marines his career, and he served in the Gulf War where he lost his left leg at the knee when his transport hit an IED. I was fifteen when he came back." Abby smiled slightly. "He was different after the war. I guess losing a leg and living through the rest of it would change you. Eventually he left the area, moved up to northern Michigan and bought a farm. I've never been there, but we've written back and forth a few times a year. You know, like at Christmas and birthdays. I haven't seen him in years, though. I've never made it up there, and he's always said he was too busy on the farm. He didn't even make it back for the funeral when Mom and Dad died in the car wreck four years ago."

Tears started to build in Abby's eyes. "I didn't know him very well, but he was the only relative I had left. At least that I know of. Uncle Gordon never married, never had kids. Sounds silly, considering that we haven't talked in ages, but I feel so alone now, knowing he is gone. I'm not really sure what to do."

Lucy watched her friend's face, the glitter of tears brightening the hazel eyes. "Well, I'd say the first thing to do would be to find a flight to... where is it... the back of beyond in Michigan, and find out what's happening." Lucy nodded her head emphatically. "Considering everything that's been going on around here, lately, getting out of Phoenix would be good for you. It would give things a chance to settle down."

Abby took a deep breath and gathered her wits. "Yeah, you're right, Lucy. I need to get out of here for a while. A little time off in Michigan could be just what I need." Abby laughed. "Who knows, I might even decide to stay."

"You. Living in the backwoods. Probably not a Starbucks in sight. Not likely," Lucy laughed at the idea.

Abby paused at the top of the steep gangway leading off the small aircraft and surveyed her surroundings. It had been a long day, flying from Phoenix to Detroit early that morning, then boarding the tiny, propeller driven Saab airplane for the final jump to Alpena, Michigan.

Upon entering the aircraft designated for that final leg of her journey, Abby nearly turned tail and ran back down the ramp, and all the way to Phoenix if necessary. Even though she had traveled a fair amount in her life, she had never been in an airplane so small. A long central aisle passed down the length of the fuselage with a series of single seats on either side that sat on small raised platforms which also ran the length of the plane.

A sense of claustrophobia temporarily halted her in the middle of the aisle, broken only when the people lined up behind began clamoring for her to move. When she reached her seat near the rear of airplane and saw her assigned spot, she was again momentarily at a loss. While only five-five, and a slight 124 pounds, she was certain she would not fit into that tiny space. She kept telling herself the seat, and everything else about the seating arrangements had to be of normal dimensions, but she just couldn't convince her lying eyes.

If the seating arrangements hadn't convinced Abby of the wisdom of renting a car and driving herself to Detroit for the return trip, the actual flight to Alpena nearly accomplished that goal. A late summer storm system had created an unstable air mass over southeastern Michigan, and the airplane's stabilizers were apparently not up to the task of holding the craft steady in the sky. It seemed to Abby that various updrafts, downdrafts, shears and, for all she knew, circular and spiral drafts all shook the plane. Several times the turbulence threatened to paste the passengers to the low ceiling, or drive them through their seats to the floor, making the ride seem more like a roller coaster than a short cross country jaunt, and made the gentle landing seem almost anticlimactic.

As she surveyed the area from the top of the steep gangway, Abby was faced with a large, glass-fronted building which appeared to be the terminal. A warm, damp breeze caught her pony tail, blowing the light brown hair over her shoulder and into her face.

Marching up to the back and sides of the building was a thick forest. Turning her head and looking back down the runway, Abby saw farm fields, surrounded by even more forest. Abby had seen forests before when she had ventured out of Phoenix to northern Arizona, but never had she seen such an abundance of trees, and she began to wonder if all of Michigan was nothing but trees and green, a green like nothing she'd ever seen before.

Abby made her way down the steep stairway and across the wet tarmac to the glass door of the terminal. Next to the building was a two-tiered luggage carrier from which people had extracted their bags on the way into the building. It only took a moment for her to locate her black, wheeled suitcase, pull it off and make her way into the terminal itself.

Halting just inside the door, Abby looked around the small area. Passengers who had already entered were either greeting friends and relatives, or making their way out of the large glass doors on the opposite side of the building to the parking lot visible beyond. Abby looked for someone who seemed to be searching as well, and finally her eyes met with those of a tall young man, who smiled and stepped forward to greet her.

"Miss Williams? Abigail Williams?"

"Yes, I'm Abigail Williams." Abby nodded at the man, smiling in return. "You must be Mr. Laskis."

"Please call me Rick." Rick thrust out his hand and took Abigail's, giving it a quick shake.

Abby appraised him quickly, taking in the boyish face under the unruly dark brown hair. His dark brown eyes sparkled in a tan face, white teeth flashing out with his smile, immediately making Abby feel at home.

"Are you ready to head out?" Rick asked. "It's about an hour's drive from here. We've got some paperwork to take care of, but we can do it at the farm."

When Abby called the lawyer from Phoenix to arrange her visit, he had said he would pick her up at the airport and drive her out to her uncle's farm. There, since she was Gordon's executor and sole beneficiary, she would have access to her uncle's house and truck for the duration of her stay, or until she decided what to do with them.

Taking a deep breath, and grabbing the handle of her suitcase, she nodded to Rick. "Let's get started, then."

4

The drive out from Alpena went quickly. Rick was a great conversationalist and willingly answered all of Abby's questions to the best of his ability.

Two weeks ago Gordon Dorsey was found floating face down in the small lake on his property. Examination indicated that Dorsey had drowned, presumably after falling and hitting his head on his dock, since there was evidence of trauma to his left temple. Several bottles which held residue of homemade beer were on his front porch, and the general consensus was that Gordon, either slightly or extremely drunk, had wandered down to the dock at night, slipped or tripped and hit his head, then fallen off the dock into the water. Either unconscious from the drink, the blow to the head, or both, he had then drowned. Water and lake bottom muck in his lungs confirmed that part, at least.

Throughout Rick's recounting Abby listened quietly while she watched the trees fly past. At times the sides of the road were so densely forested that she felt as though she were driving through a long green tunnel. Then suddenly they'd emerge into an area of farmland; fields showing evidence of the approaching fall harvest. Then, just as quickly, they'd dive back between the trees again.

Finally, Rick ground to a halt and silence reigned in the car for several minutes as Abby digested what she had been told. Abby looked at Rick's profile as he studied the road ahead of him then she took a deep breath.

"Did you know my uncle well?"

"Well, I was his lawyer for about a year. However, I met him about four years ago when I moved to the area." Rick's lips quirked in a smile at the memory.

"How did you meet him?"

"I met him at the Alpena Farmer's Market. I used to buy fish from him, as well as some fruit and vegetables during the right seasons."

"A farmer's market? Fish?" Abby was floored by the revelation. "What type of farmer was my uncle, exactly?"

"What did he tell you?" Rick laughed at her reaction.

"Well, we didn't communicate a lot. Just letters or Christmas cards once a year or so." Abby looked out the car window for a moment, thinking. Suddenly she laughed. "When I'd write to him, I'd always say I hoped all was going well with the farm, and he'd always answer that things were fine as long as the fish were biting. I just thought that he was totally into fishing."

Rick glanced at her, a grin splitting his face. "In a way he was. He was one of the only small trout farms in the area, and he was the only one who used all organic feed for his fish. He'd produce trout for himself, then sell any extra at the farmer's market, or to private customers. He has a few cattle, some chickens and a couple of goats as well, but his main income as far as livestock went, was trout."

"Was it one of those 'come and fish and pay for what you catch' things?"

"No, your uncle was a bit of a loner. He didn't welcome a lot of people to the farm. I went and fished with him a few times, but mostly, he'd net the trout, clean them and take them to the market on ice. He was considering trying a live tank, but hadn't gotten that far. He also had several hotels and restaurants which would buy from him. It made him a fair little income."

"You said that you met him about four years ago, but

didn't become his lawyer until the last year. What happened?"

"A couple of things." A slight frown creased Rick's profile. "It started when Gordon found out he had cancer."

"What!?" Abby stared at Rick's profile, her hazel eyes wide and shocked.

"Yeah. Lung cancer. We'd talked at the farmer's market, so he knew I was a lawyer. When he found out he had cancer, he decided he needed to get things in order, so that when... that when... well, you know. He didn't want the farm going into probate... wanted to make it as easy a transition as possible for you."

Abby was silent for a moment, chewed on her lower lip and pulled on a lock of her tawny brown hair as she stared out the window at the ranks of trees flying past. Taking a deep breath, she looked at Rick, who was concentrating on the road, considerately giving her time to deal with her emotions in as much privacy as a car would allow.

"You said a couple of things. What else was going on?"

"You uncle was being pressured to sell his farm. He wasn't interested, but then some allegations arose over the products he was taking to the farmer's market and he was concerned that the person trying to buy the farm was spreading rumors in order to damage his business and try to force him to sell. Not much came of it, since the complaints were made anonymously but he did notice fewer people buying for a time, and a couple of the restaurants questioned him."

Suddenly Abby's phone chirped, indicating that it had a new message. Surprised, since she hadn't heard it ring, she quickly checked the screen. Scowling she hit the dismiss button, effectively silencing the device. As the phone returned to its normal wallpaper, she noticed that there were very few bars in evidence, and those that were shown tended to blink in and out.

"You don't get very good reception in this area, do you?"

"No, northern Michigan isn't really high on the cell phone providers list of 'must serve' areas." Rick chuckled. "It's quite a shock for a lot of people coming up here for vacation from down south."

Abby took a deep breath. "So now the farm is mine. I know I'm his only relative, but I guess I'm sort of surprised that he left it to me. After all, I'm not a farmer."

Rick glanced quickly at Abby, meeting her eyes briefly before returning his concentration to the road ahead.

"Oh, he thought you had potential."

"He did?"

"Yeah. He talked about you pretty proudly; how you were some big advertising executive and everything. But he said there was something in you that called for the outdoors, although you didn't know it yet."

Abby stared at the road ahead of her, at a loss for something to say. The idea that her uncle, whom she'd seldom talked to, and hadn't seen in years, thought that she belonged here boggled the mind. She wondered if it was wishful thinking on the part of an old man with only one relative, or if he had truly intuited something about her which she herself didn't even realize existed. Gradually she became aware of a growing excitement and curiosity to see if Uncle Gordon had been right.

Wow, thought Abby. Her mind blanked of all ideas but that one word. *Wow.*

They'd been traveling down a small two-lane road designated a "county road" in this area, delving deeper into the "forest primeval" as she'd come to think of the thick undergrowth of northern Michigan woods. With almost no warning Rick turned off the narrow blacktopped thoroughfare onto an even smaller dirt road, where the canopy of the trees met over the center and she felt as though she were transported to another world altogether.

Few people lived on this road, at least that she could see. Twice they passed some farms where the trees were cleared and she could see cattle, crops and ponds set off in the distance. After about four miles they came to a small brown double-wide tucked back into the forest with a large steel workshop in the back. They slowed and turned on the small gravel driveway to the left of the buildings.

Abby was confused, since it looked nothing like a farm in her estimation. She turned to ask Rick but they had already driven past the trailer following the narrow lane into the thick undergrowth behind the workshop. A few seconds later they came out into wide open pasture land surrounded by trees. In the distance to the left she could see an old white-washed barn with a green shingled, gambrel roof. To the right she could see a cedar and field stone house set back in the trees, the glint of a small lake shining beyond.

"Here we are," Rick said. He glanced over at Abby, as if to gauge her reaction to the sight. The sky had been overcast when Abby arrived in Alpena, but the clouds were starting to break up and chunks of blue shown through the gray, allowing errant rays of sunshine to fall on the fields and barn.

Abby looked at Rick, her eyes wide in awe. "This is Uncle Gordon's farm?" she asked, almost to herself as it was obvious that it must be. Otherwise they wouldn't have been there. She realized she'd never even seen a picture of the farm before. She and Gordon had corresponded over the years, but not a great deal, and he certainly hadn't been into the internet/Facebook culture that pervaded everything these days. She wasn't even sure if he had a computer.

Thinking back, Abby realized that the only pictures she'd ever seen had been close-ups of animals, or of the lake, and very few of even those subjects had made their way to her door. She'd simply never realized the wonder of what her uncle had built here and suddenly she missed him more than she ever thought possible considering the tenuous nature of their contact in recent years.

"Yep," Rick said as he pulled into the wide graveled yard between the house and the barn. "He put a lot of time and work into this place. He said when he bought it the fields were overrun, the barn was in poor shape, and the house was a shell, unsafe to live in."

"But it's beautiful now," Abby protested, nodding toward the cozy two-story structure perched on a hill leading down to the small lake."

"That's not the original house. The original owners built the house over closer to the main road. Less of a driveway to clear out when it snowed, I guess." Rick grinned at her. "You haven't seen some of our Michigan snows. They're the things snow birds are made of," he said, referring to the habit common to some people of spending the summer months in a northern climate, and then hightailing it for places like Florida and Arizona during the winter. He laughed at the expression of horror on her face at the thought. "A lot of people build close to the road so that they have less plowing."

"I guess Gordon wasn't too worried about snow," Abby said as she looked back down the length of driveway leading to the house and barn.

"No, he didn't have the same need," Rick said, opening the car door and starting to unfold his long legs. "He didn't run a dairy farm, so the milk truck didn't have to make it in every morning, and...," Rick grinned back at Abby, "he also said that he'd just as soon not make it too easy for people to come in and pester him."

"Well, I guess he managed that. You can't even see this place from the road."

"I was told that when this place was first farmed the

only road frontage that it had was down in a swampy area. The original owners were able to buy an easement from the residents of the property out front, and it was cheaper to go in that direction for the driveway." Rick opened his door, climbed out and stretched, arms skyward. On the other side of the car Abby emerged, groaning at the twinge of muscles cramped from a long day of traveling, and surveyed her new domain.

"Now, of course, Gordon bought that property as well, so the easement isn't really an issue any longer. He rents the house we passed to Adam Thomas. He's the man who helped Gordon with the farm in exchange for part of the rent, and it was actually he who found the body." Rick paused, looking around as if searching for something or someone.

"Actually, there he is now." Rick gestured toward the large sliding door of the barn from which a young man was emerging with two white five-gallon buckets, and a rope attached to an excited black, tan and white dog.

Adam put down one of his buckets and lifted his hand to wave to Rick and Abby, then set the other bucket down and made his way over to them.

Rick smiled and waved, saying over his shoulder, "Adam has been taking care of the place since Gordon passed away. He's always helped Gordon so he just took over all the chores; feeding the animals and the fish, and taking care of Max."

Adam drew closer, and the dog at his side became more animated, trying to free itself from the piece of rope tied to its collar.

"Hi guys," Adam said, then "Oops!" as he tripped over the dog for the fifth time. "Max, settle down. You must be Abigail," Adam nodded toward Abby, a welcoming smile on his tanned face.

"Call me Abby," Abby smiled back at Adam, his cheerful disposition contagious. "What a beautiful dog. What's its name?"

"It's Max. Actually it's Gordon's dog. Although I've been taking her home with me the last couple of weeks since... since... I mean, since your uncle passed away." A cloud covered Adam's face as he remembered the reason for Abby's arrival. His dark, almost black eyes were filled with sorrow.

"Her? *Her* name is Max?" Abby said.

"Yeah. Short for Maxine according to Gordon." Adam bent down to untie the rope from Max's collar. "Usually she just runs free around here. I've never known her to leave the place. Hell, she'll hardly leave Gordon's side. Uh, I guess I mean she'd hardly leave his side." Adam gave a bitter laugh. "But since he died she's been doing some really weird stuff. Carrying strange things around, sitting down at the lake for hours, trying to take off down the road, arguing more." Adam shook his head. "I'm worried about her. She and Gordon were inseparable."

Abby knelt as Max approached her, eyes fixed on Abby's in a disconcerting manner. Abby stretched out her hand to scratch the dog's ears, but Max stopped just out of reach, continuing to stare at Abby.

Abby gave a self-conscious laugh and dropped her hand onto her knee, rising back to a standing position. "Arguing? What do you mean arguing?"

Rick chuckled at the obvious disbelief in Abby's voice and Adam's sunny expression returned as a huge grin split his face.

"Well, you see...," Rick started.

"When you tell Max to do something she doesn't agree with, she argues with you," Adam continued.

"Seriously?" Abby looked from Rick to Adam, then back at Max, meeting that intense stare once more. She felt an uncomfortable urge to look away, to look anywhere but into those golden brown and blue eyes.

"Yeah, seriously." Adam's grin grew wider. "It's hilarious to watch. Not quite so hilarious when you realize that someone else is watching you argue with a dog."

"So, you're argumentative, huh?" Abby said softly to Max.

Max replied with a soft woof. More breath than sound, but it was obvious that she was responding to Abby's comment and those disconcerting eyes never left Abby's face.

"What do you argue about? Brand of dog? Types of chewy toys?"

Another soft woof, followed by a sneeze, as if Max were showing contempt at Abby's statement.

"Well, as a matter of fact," said Adam, "she tends to argue about more important stuff. Try telling her that you're going into town without her sometime, or that she can't come fishing, and you'll get the argument of the century, and the odds are you'll lose."

Abby broke eye contact with the dog and looked at the two men standing with her in the barnyard.

The barnyard she now owned.

"Okay. I'll take your comments under advisement. Now it's getting late, and I know you need to get back into town, Rick, so what exactly do we need to get done this afternoon?"

A few hours later, will read and papers signed, Abby found herself alone in the front room of the house. She looked around the bright, spacious open area, appreciating the natural pine and oak woodwork that made up the floors, window frames and ceiling of the structure. Rick told her that Gordon had built much of the house himself or with the help of Adam and a few other people in the area, hiring licensed contractors for those few tasks with which he felt unqualified.

The main floor of the house had an open design, with the kitchen flowing into a dining area, and hanging a right into a full length living room area bordered by floor to ceiling windows. A half bath and small bedroom sat across a short hallway from the kitchen itself. Two steep staircases led out of the living room. One headed upward to the second floor where two bedrooms and the main bathroom were located, and one down to a walk-in basement which housed a shop, another full bath, and a small entertainment room, which in her uncle's case meant a TV, DVD player and nothing else. A door on the left side of the main floor led outside to a walk-though screened porch which flowed around the front of a house to a large half-octagon deck with an amazing view of the tiny lake.

Feeling at a loss, Abby turned and made her way down the short hall between the kitchen and the bathroom and out the back door then headed off across the driveway toward the barn. An old green Jeep had joined Adam's red truck parked in front of the open door, and Abby could hear voices and laughter emanating from that cavernous space.

The late summer weather had turned warm and humid, but upon entering the barn the temperature seemed to drop ten degrees. The smell of dust, hay and animals met her nose as she paused to let her eyes adjust to the dark interior of the barn. She found herself in a large central alleyway, facing an old red tractor. In the shadowy depths of the barn she could see other pieces of equipment which she couldn't identify. Above her head was a low wooden ceiling with an open trapdoor, showing a glimpse of the hay stored above. On either side of the ally, wooden walls with doors hinted at more space to either side of the barn. Probably, Abby thought, for housing the animals in the winter.

Abby could hear the voices coming from a partially open door on the left and headed in that direction. She stepped into a large room with concrete floors and a big window letting in the evening sun. Adam was there, scooping feed into a series of buckets and talking to a young woman milking a large brown goat. A long haired calico cat was sitting at the woman's feet. Max was sitting next to Adam, but at the sight of Abby in the doorway, she jumped up and ran over, still staying just out of her reach. Adam looked up at Max's reaction and smiled a welcome.

"Hi, Abby. Come on in. We're just doing the evening chores." Adam nodded toward the young woman. "Abby, this is my girlfriend, Jenn. Jennifer Painter. She runs a consignment store and art gallery in Onaway, but she's been helping me here since your uncle's death. The goat is Autumn and the fur ball on the floor is Cali Cat. Your uncle had a way with naming his animals, that's for sure." Adam's dark brown eyes sparkled with laughter

"Hi Jenn." Abby smiled at the young woman, noting

how her bright blue eyes seemed to almost glow in the dimness of the room. Her shoulder-length blonde hair was tied back into a pony tail, and she wore an old t-shirt, shorts and sneakers which had seen better days. "I'm so glad to meet you. Thank you for helping on my uncle's farm."

"It's nice to meet you too, Abby." Jenn said in a soft voice, right hand absently stroking the side of the goat next to her. "I'm sorry about your uncle. He was such a nice guy."

"Thanks. I guess I didn't know him well. We'd only been writing to each other a few times a year, so it's good to hear how much everyone liked him."

Abby moved further into the room, Max shadowing her every move.

"What's with the dog? She doesn't seem to like me, but she won't leave me alone either." Abby looked down only to find those disturbingly intelligent eyes fixed on her face again. Abby gave a self-conscious laugh. "I feel like I'm on trial and the jury is still out."

Adam nodded toward Max. "You probably are on trial. She's an Australian Shepherd. They're one of the smartest breeds out there, and Max is at the top of the pack as far as brains go.

"Gordon got her as a three week old pup. Too young to leave her mother, but the people who owned the dam hadn't planned on a litter at that time and weren't even sure what dog was the father, although it was probably another Aussie from the looks of Max.

"They decided they didn't want to deal with puppies and showed up at the farmer's market one weekend, selling them for twenty-five dollars. When Gordon found out he was furious. Max was the only puppy left, the runt of the litter, and he said he took her just to make sure that she got decent care. He had to bottle feed her at the beginning, she was so tiny. We found out later that most of the other pups people bought that day died from one thing or another; mostly parvo. Max is the only one we know of who survived."

Abby looked at Max again. "So, you're a miracle puppy, huh?" That same soft woof with more breath than sound, eyes never leaving Abby's face. The dog's bobbed tail jerked from side to side once. Not really a wag, but it was something.

Jenn smiled, "Well, she's your miracle now. She belongs to you."

Abby frowned. "Surely she'd be happier with you guys. She doesn't even seem to trust me. Besides, what would I do with a dog like her in Phoenix? She'd hate it."

Adam looked at her, for once no smile on his face. He glanced at Jenn, then ran his hand through his short-cropped dark hair.

"You're not planning on staying then?"

"I just came up to take care of the paperwork and check things out. I guess I'll probably be selling the farm. I've got no idea how to run it, and I've got a job waiting for me back in the Valley."

Adam took a deep breath and looked back at Jenn, then down at the floor. "I see. I guess we were hoping that you were going to come in and keep the farm going. We've enjoyed living here. It's been a good place, and there aren't a lot of small farms left."

Abby looked at the two in front of her. "I don't suppose you'd want to buy it yourselves?"

Adam shook his head. "Nah. Way out of our league. There are a lot of people wanting this place, if only for the cabin and lake. Gordon was always turning down offers, from both farmers and developers." A sad smile crossed his face as his eyes met Jenn's across the room.

"I suppose it's just natural to hope things would stay the same. I guess I'd better get on with the chores." He turned back to the feed bin and started dishing up more pellets of some type into the buckets at his feet. Abby looked down, and for the first time realized that there was something about Adam's right leg that wasn't natural. His jean's leg had pulled up over his hiking boot a little and she caught the glint of a prosthetic limb. Adam finished filling the buckets, and started to turn, catching Abby's gaze on his leg. Twitching the denim back over the top of his boot, he smiled a bit sadly.

"I lost it in Afghanistan. IED. I was lucky on that mission. I only lost my leg. Others lost more." He grimaced and shook his head. "I came back a bit messed up. They call it PTSD; post-traumatic stress disorder. I met your uncle at the VA in Oscoda. I guess we sort of bonded in the prosthetics' department. He lost his left leg, and I lost my right, so we used to say that between us we had two good legs and could do anything." Adam's smile brightened at the welcomed memory. "He heard that I was struggling, and offered me the house up by the road. Said I could help him with the cabin and chores in exchange for part of the rent, and he'd help me get on my feet again, so to say."

Abby's heart broke. "Well, I've got a month before I have to be back at work. Maybe a good option will present itself and things won't have to change too much." She grinned at Adam and Jenn. "Meanwhile, you guys better teach me what you can about being a country girl. I'm used to all my food coming from the grocery store. I've got a feeling that 'farmer's market' doesn't have the same meaning here as it did in Phoenix."

"Alright then," Adam grinned. "Let's start with feeding the fish." Adam handed her a pair of buckets and led the way out of the big double doors.

The pair headed up the hill behind the barn, making for several large weeping willows, Max running alongside. Abby had noticed that area earlier, but hadn't connected it with anything. For some reason, in her mind, when Rick said that Gordon had been farming trout, she had just assumed that said trout would be in the lake in front of the cabin. Instead she and Adam were headed the opposite direction from the lake.

They followed a well-worn trail for about 200 yards until they reached the willows. As the pair drew closer, Abby could see that the trees shaded several ponds, all connected to one another by a series of channels and dams, small waterfalls moving the water from one pond to another. Drawing up to the lowest of the ponds, Abby set her bucket on the ground, breathing hard.

"Why on earth did my uncle decide to build his fish farm up here? Was he some sort of masochist and wanted to carry food up here all the time?"

"I wasn't here when he first put it in, but I'm told that it was an accident in a way."

"How could it be an accident?"

"From what I was told, Gordon never planned on farming fish when he bought the place. He was just looking for a place to call his own, and he got a good deal on the property. The old well had caved in, so he needed to drill a new one. He got a dowser to come out and help him choose the location."

"What the heck is a dowser?"

"Someone who uses a dowsing rod, or sometimes a pendulum, to search for water. They walk around and when they're in a good spot to drill, the tip of the wand dips down."

"You've got to be kidding me. There are people who do that?" Abby looked at Adam in surprise.

Adam laughed at the incredulous look on her face. "Yeah, there are people who do that, and some of them are really good. A lot of property owners rely on them. Anyway, the dowser told Gordon that there was good water in this area. Problem is that when they drilled they hit an artesian aquifer."

Abby felt like she'd entered another world with a whole new language. "Okay, what is an artesian aquifer? I've heard of artesian spring water. People pay big bucks for it in the stores. I've worked on a couple of advertising accounts for them, but just thought it was some ultra-pure spring water."

"That's what all those advertising types would like you to believe." Adam looked at her out of the corner of his eye. His voice held a teasing note which made Abby smile. "Actually, an artesian aquifer is an aquifer which is under pressure. So, if there is a natural break in the rock, you might wind up with an artesian spring. If you drill a well down into it, you might wind up with a flowing well, or a flowing artesian well. Since the water is under pressure, it's pushed up without needing a pump. Water runs all the time. They can be a pain, and they waste a lot of ground water in the government's estimation, so there are now regulations surrounding them and instruments used to control the flow.

"So, Gordon was faced with this flowing well, and looking for something to farm. Other artesian wells have been used by trout hatcheries around the state, so he decided why not. Turned out the water was of excellent quality, and the flow rate and temperature were perfect. Gordon likes trout, so he became a trout farmer.

"Now, we need to make sure that all the feeders are full. Trout eat a lot, and most of these older fish are using demand feeders. We just need to make sure they're kept full so that when the trout move the lever, they get the food."

Abby was floored. "You mean that the fish can learn to feed themselves? They're that smart?"

Adam was pulling in a feeder from the middle of a dirt sided pond with a dam at either end. "Yeah, the larger fish do well with it, at least here. We use a different type of automatic feeder for the juveniles and fingerlings."

Abby was looking at Adam with a shell shocked expression.

"It's not really a big deal, Abby," Adam said, smiling. "You'll get the hang of it pretty quickly. Why don't you go up to the next pond and fill that feeder." Adam gestured toward another long, narrow dirt pond, attached to the first one by a dam with a trapdoor and grate which allowed water to flow through and drop into the next enclosure, the small waterfall it created causing the water to boil up.

Abby grabbed her buckets and headed to the spot that Adam indicated, and started pulling in the floating feeder the way she saw him do at the first pond. The two worked in companionable silence for several minutes, Abby enjoying the peaceful sounds of the falling water, and the birds settling down for the evening.

As the two headed back down to the barn Abby looked around at the idyllic surroundings. "Adam, do you believe that my uncle was drunk when he died?" Abby asked. The question had been nagging at her since Rick had first told her how her uncle had been found.

Adam studied the ground ahead of him, as if thinking about his answer. Finally taking a deep breath he said, "I don't know, Abby. I found him, and the beer bottles were on the deck, but there's something wrong." Adam frowned as he contemplated the question.

"I knew your uncle over six years, and never once during all that time did I ever see him drunk. He'd have a beer occasionally, sure, and he was playing with some brewing using local fruits, but drunk? I just don't see it."

"No," Abby said. "My mother told me about how he struggled when he returned from the Gulf War. She said he was on pain killers, and was drinking heavy on top of that. It took some doing, but she said he got himself straightened out and cleaned up. From what I know of him, I have a really hard time believing that he went back to the bottle like that."

"There was the cancer," Adam said softly, almost to himself. "But he said he wasn't giving up and that he was going to fight it. I guess I really want to believe that he hadn't given up, because if he gave up, what does that mean for me? I mean if I am faced with a challenge in the future?"

"He didn't give up," Abby said with determination. She looked over at Adam as they came to a stop in front of the barn. "I know he didn't. But if he wasn't drunk, then how did he come to fall in the water? Did the police investigate at all?"

"The sheriff's department was called, and they investigated, but it seemed like a pretty open and shut case. Accidental death. I guess he could have just tripped on the dock and hit his head, but it just doesn't feel right." Adam's eyes met hers, a question and a plea obvious in them.

"Well, that's it then, Adam. I'll call the sheriff's department tomorrow and talk with the deputy in charge of the investigation. Maybe we just need some fresh eyes on the situation."

Abby was in the water, thrashing around, trying to get to the dock which seemed to get farther and farther away the more she thrashed. She tried to scream, but her mouth filled with water and she couldn't breathe. She started to cough and cough and...

Abby jerked to wakefulness, a long, calico tail brushing her face and making her cough and sneeze. In the dim light of early morning she rolled her eyes up to look at the bookshelf headboard of the bed in which she was sleeping. Attached to the calico tail was, predictably, the small calico body of Cali Cat. A small white paw extended and patted Abby on the forehead and the large glowing golden green eyes examined her face. Abby brushed the tail out of her mouth and rolled over with an *umph* and closed her eyes again. Whatever time it was, if it was still dark it was entirely too early to be getting up.

An uncomfortable feeling started to itch at the back of her neck. She ignored it and tried to force herself back to sleep. After minutes which seemed like an eternity she finally gave up and opened her eyes again, only to gasp and jerk backward.

The edge of the bed was a few scant inches away from her nose and sitting on the floor, immediately in front of her face, was Max, intense golden brown and blue eyes fixed on hers. Again.

Abby jerked into a sitting position, her heart pounding. "What the... Max! You scared the hell out of me!"

A soft woof.

"That's all you can say? Woof?" Abby reached out her hand, and once again Max ducked away from her outstretched fingers.

Gradually Abby's heart rate returned to normal and she slumped against the headboard. All thought of sleep was banished from her mind and instead she contemplated her current situation. She was in a strange place, being watched by a strange dog and she had this uncomfortable feeling that she was just touching the tip of the iceberg of the strangeness yet to come.

Max uttered another soft woof.

"Did you want something?"

To Abby's surprise, Max lifted her nose and emitted a combination of sounds that weren't a bark, weren't a howl, and seemed disturbingly to be in answer to her question. The problem was that she didn't understand the language.

"Sorry I didn't get that. Do you mind repeating?"

Another long string of yodeling syllables, this time punctuated by a sharp bark at the end. Max spun around and headed out the door, then turned back to face Abby again.

Abby stared at the dog, mouth hanging open in astonishment. Max, apparently annoyed by Abby's apparent lack of understanding, voiced another series of sounds, whirled again and headed out the door and down the stairs. Cali Cat padded softly after her, tail waving gently from side to side.

"Alright, then," Abby muttered to herself, throwing the blankets back and swinging her legs out of the bed. "Looks like Timmy is in the well again, Lassie."

Abby followed Max down the steep stairs and to the side door where the dog waited impatiently.

"I guess you want out?"

A soft woof, followed by a louder, sharper bark, eyes

fixed on Abby's face the entire time.

"Okay, then. I guess when a girl's gotta go, a girl's gotta go." Abby reached over the dog and opened the door. Max ran out and headed toward the barn, closely followed by Cali Cat. Peering out into the dim morning light, Abby saw the dog and cat disappear through the open door. There were no vehicles in front of the structure, so that probably meant that Adam hadn't come to start morning chores yet but she figured it wouldn't be in the too distant future and she had a long list of things to do. Turning she headed back across the living area and up the steep staircase, the cool morning air brushed across her bare legs and raised goose bumps on her arms. First thing on the agenda, bathroom and hot shower. Then coffee. A lot of coffee.

Not long afterward Abby was sitting on the deck, snuggled into an old fleece pullover of her uncle's as she enjoyed her second cup of coffee, and the sight of the lake in equal measure. An eerie sound floated across the water, one familiar from all those spooky horror movies she'd watched when she was younger; the soundtrack to terror as she remembered it. The loons. Both Adam and Rick had mentioned that there was a pair which had nested across the lake from the dock in the deep weeds along the shore. This late in the summer their chicks were well on the way to adulthood. However they continued to use the lake as home base, fishing in it, and out into the nearby river. She had yet to see them but their calls punctuated her night's sleep, scaring her at first, then calming, lulling her back to her slumbers.

She heard a truck engine rumbling up the long driveway. Rising and stretching, she headed across the deck, and down the steps to the trail leading around toward the back of the house.

Adam's old Ford pickup was parked in front of the barn and he was heading in through the open door. Abby called out and waved her hand, causing him to turn and look back toward the house.

"Hey, Abby. Good morning. Hope you slept well."

Abby jogged across the barnyard to catch up with him. "I slept okay I guess, although I'm not sure about the feline canine tag team wakeup call this morning.

"The what?" Adam looked momentarily puzzled, and then saw Max and Cali Cat approaching from the back of the barn. "Oh. I get it. Gordon always said that Max's internal clock was even better than his, and his was good. She likes to start every day checking out the farm and making sure that everything survived the night in her absence."

"Well, she did that, and now I'm ready to do the same, I guess. I suppose you should show me all the chores, and introduce me to how this place works. I only got to meet the fish and the goat last night. I suppose I need to learn what I have before I figure out what to do with it." Abby smiled at Adam.

"Sounds good to me," Adam said, smiling in return. "Let's start with the cattle and the horses."

An hour and a half later Abby's head was spinning and Adam seemed to be enjoying her discomfort.

"So, let me go over it again. The cows are Emily and Annabelle. Emily is Annabelle's mother, even though Annabelle is twice the size of Emily. And they have calves every year which are either sold or butchered."

"Yep. Emily was an orphaned calf that one of Gordon's friends gave him. He raised her on a bottle."

"Then we've got the goats. Autumn is a milk goat, and Rose, Lilly and Daisy are Boar goats, which are for meat. They each have..." Abby searched her mind for the right term."...kids every year which are either sold or butchered, as well."

"Good job! The goats aren't too much trouble, unless they get loose of course. Then you're going to be having fun because even though Autumn is gentle, the flowers are pretty wild, and their kids are even wilder. They enjoy jumping on everything that stands still enough which can make catching them an adventure."

"Then there's Bella, the big white dog, whose job it is to guard all the critters in the pasture from wild animals. And the horses are Grace and Hope, and they really don't have any job but to stand around, eat hay and look pretty. Add in the chickens with no names, and the fish. Good grief, Adam, what in the world am I going to do?"

Adam shrugged and shook his head. "I don't know Abby. I guess you'll do whatever you think is right." He fished in his pocket for a set of keys. "But right now what I'm going to do is get to work. I've gotten a bit behind since your uncle passed away so I'd better hop to it. I'll come back around four-thirty or five and help you with the evening chores." He headed for his truck.

Abby followed him, feeling surprised. "I thought you worked here. I mean on the farm. That you helped my uncle in exchange for rent?"

"I do, but he also helped me get set up in my own business. Sometimes he needed me more here, like when it was time to put in some hay, process a bunch of fish or do repairs on the tractor or the barn. Other times I pay my bills as an independent welder and mechanic." Adam laughed at Abby's surprised expression. "I told you that Gordon said he'd help me get on my feet. I use that workshop behind my house as my home base, but I also have a mobile set up, so if someone breaks down out on the road or in the field, and it's something relatively simple, I can get them going again without the tow.

"Normally a place like ours would rent for seven hundred to nine hundred dollars a month, or more considering the workshop. Gordon charges... charged me only three hundred dollars a month, the rest to be taken out in labor. It's been a good deal for both of us."

"I can see that," Abby said thoughtfully.

"You know, if you decide you want to stay here you could learn everything you need to know. It's a good place here. Good people."

"Adam, I can't stay here. I don't know how to run this place. For pete's sake, I'm in advertising not agriculture!"

"You could do that here, you know. Michigan companies advertise also."

Abby bit the inside of her lip, thinking. Things had become uncomfortable in Phoenix recently, with the Josh situation and all. She didn't always see eye to eye with the new management at her company, either. She had considered opening her own business, going back to her roots as a web designer, but not at the back end of nowhere.

"There isn't internet in the house!" Abby said. "Good grief, there isn't even reliable cell service up here. How could I run a business where I need to be able to contact people, develop web content. It's not doable, Adam." She clenched her teeth in frustration.

"It's not the moon, Abby. Gordon didn't want internet. That doesn't mean it isn't available. He said there wasn't much out there that he really needed to know. He has a TV and DVD player in the basement, probably because they were given to him. He'd rather read a book or go fishing than watch TV, so I really wouldn't be surprised to find out that a mouse had set up residence in the guts of the DVD player. I'd be careful when I turned it on if I were you."

"Not a good way to instill confidence. I sure hope that Cali Cat is more than a pretty face and furry butt."

"She's packed in more than her fair share of rodents since Gordon picked her up at the grocery store." Adam grinned at the shocked expression on Abby's face. "Just think about staying. You can make it work, I know you can."

"I can't say anything more than I'll think about it. Heck, I haven't even been here twenty-four hours. I need to get a chance to catch my breath." *And I need to find out if my uncle had help going into the water,* she thought. "By the way, who investigated my uncle's death? I mean what department?"

"The Presque Isle County Sheriff's Department. That's who came when I called 911, and before you say anything, yes there is a 911. Since they felt it was a pretty run of the mill accidental death, it stopped there. From what I hear, the body has been released and everyone was just waiting for you to decide what to do about a funeral or memorial." He slipped in behind the steering wheel and fished for the ignition.

"Okay, I'll get started on that today, but I definitely want to talk to someone at the department to see if they even looked at the possibility of something other than accidental death."

"Sounds like you've got a fun day ahead of you," Adam said, turning the key and putting the truck into reverse. "I'll leave you to it. If you need me, I'll be up at the shop. I gave you my number last night, right?"

"Yup," Abby answered, already so deep in thought that she didn't even wave as Adam drove off down the road.

First things first, thought Abby, heading back toward the house, Max following behind like a shadow. *I need to find a phone book and call the sheriff's department to find out who investigated my uncle's death.* "Come on Max, we've got some work to do."

Her shadow emitted a sharp bark, as she ran past Abby and around the corner of the cabin headed, as far as Abby knew, down to the lake. Abby stood there in surprise.

"Max. Max! Come here. Come Max." Abby called. Adam said that she usually ran loose on the place with no problem, but he'd also said that she'd been behaving strangely since Gordon's death.

"Geez dog," Abby muttered, changed her direction and headed around the cabin in search of the missing canine. Just as she rounded the corner of the deck aiming for the dock, she met Max running back in the opposite direction. In her mouth she carried a dirty, soggy piece of material. She ran up and pushed the rag into Abby's leg.

Abby recoiled in revulsion, but Max persisted in shoving her nose toward Abby, making it clear that she was to take the treasure. Gingerly Abby reached out and Max dropped a soggy piece of flannel into her hand. Abby grimaced at the feel, but gripped the gift firmly. Initially it appeared to be a rag. Probably something that Gordon used to clean the windows, she thought, but on closer inspection she realized that it was a sleeve of some type. It apparently came off a heavy, dark green flannel shirt, and was torn raggedly from the shoulder.

Max was sitting in front of Abby, staring at her once again.

Geez, she thought, she was getting tired of being examined by a dog, and one she couldn't even touch on top of it all. It was giving her an inferiority complex!

"Do you want me to throw this?" Abby asked Max, feeling self-conscious about talking to the dog.

A sharp bark answered her this time, not the usual soft woof.

"Alright. And what is that supposed to mean?" Abby asked frustrated.

Nose in the air, Max uttered a stream of sounds similar to the ones she'd used that morning. Abby was beginning to see what Adam had meant the night before when he said that Max was argumentative, and that it was funny to watch, but not so humorous to be involved in.

Wadding up the material, Abby threw it into the forest and waited to see what the dog would do. Max looked at Abby, then toward the woods where she had thrown the sleeve, then turned and ran through the undergrowth, retrieved the cloth and returned to Abby, shoving it at her again.

Okay, thought Abby, *she's just any dog wanting to play fetch.* She reached out for the material again, but this time Max refused to let go. Instead she just sat and held on to one end of the sleeve while Abby gripped the other.

"So, drop it," Abby commanded. No response.

"Let go?" Abby tried. Again no response. Max continued to sit in front of her, hanging on to the cloth.

"Fine, you annoying dog," Abby said in frustration, and let go of her end of the sleeve. Immediately Max tried to push the cloth back into Abby's hand.

"Dang it, Max. Fine, give it to me. I won't throw it again." Cautiously Max let the material drop from her mouth, never taking her eyes of Abby. Abby found herself holding the dilapidated sleeve once again, and tried to decide what to do with it. Finally, she folded it up, turned and headed back into the house. Setting the cloth on the counter, she began opening drawers looking for a phone book, or something that would yield the phone number of the county sheriff's office in Rogers City.

Eventually, in the third drawer she located a three year old phone book. Since she doubted that the sheriff's office had moved during the past three years, she turned to the government section and looked up the non-emergency number for Presque Isle County's law enforcement.

Dressing for late August in Michigan is certainly different than dressing for late August in Phoenix, Abby thought, going through the clothes she brought with her. Back home she'd still be wearing sleeveless shirts, shorts and sandals. Here, not so much. The early morning air had a nip in it. When she'd dressed to go outside that morning, she'd grabbed the fleece pullover her uncle had left hanging on a peg by the back door, but she wasn't sure she wanted to go into town dressed in her uncle's clothes. It appeared she would have to do a bit of shopping if she were going to stay long in Michigan. Either that, or develop a lot thicker skin, and much thicker blood.

Finally she gave up the hunt, and pulled on a pair of clean jeans, hiking boots, a blue long-sleeved t-shirt she found in her uncle's drawer, and his fleece pullover. If she was lucky, she thought, the day would warm up, and she'd be able to take off the pullover before she met with the sheriff's deputy.

Heading out to the old Dodge Dakota pickup parked behind the house, she grabbed her uncle's keys from the counter and carefully locked the door. A movement in the front seat of the truck caught the corner of her eye, causing her to pause for a moment, then approach more carefully. As she reached the dark green vehicle with no other signs of life, she began to relax, thinking she must have imagined that flicker of movement or it was a reflection in the glass. Suddenly a furry black, white and tan head popped into view from the front seat. Abby screamed and jumped backward, nearly tripping and falling. She caught her balance and stood for a second, glaring at the face that appeared in the driver's side window.

"Max! How did you get in there?" Max just looked at her, apparently not feeling the need to answer. Abby studied the truck, and noticed that the passenger window was rolled down. Max must have been able to jump in through that window, she thought, and walked around to the other side of the truck. Sure enough, while not many, a few scratches showed where Max had occasionally used her back feet to finish propelling herself in through the opening.

Walking back to the driver's side, Abby opened the door.

"Okay, Max. Good trick. Now it's time to get out. I need to go into town to meet with a deputy about Uncle Gordon's death."

Max looked at Abby and blinked, then scooted herself over to the passenger side of the seat.

"No, Max. You can't come. Get out."

Max didn't budge. Abby walked around to the passenger side of the truck and opened the door. Max, watching her, slid between the seats and into the back seat of the extended cab truck.

"Dammit, Max! I need to go. Get out of the truck now!"

Max sat behind the driver's seat, simply looking at Abby in an infuriatingly calm manner.

"Fine, you animated dust bunny." Abby shut the passenger door rather heavily, although she told herself she absolutely had *not* slammed it. She walked back to the driver's side, knowing what would happen. Sure enough, Max scooted over to the passenger side of the truck. Abby slid into the truck, started the engine, put the truck into gear and headed out the driveway, teeth gritted.

As she came up to Adam's house, she could see him working in front of the workshop; a brightly lit torch in his hands, sparks flying over the gravel. She pulled over and stopped the truck, opened the door and got out. She stood there for a moment holding the door open and waiting for him to notice her.

It only took a moment before Adam looked up and realized he was being watched.

"Hey, Abby," he called, waving. "Just a second. Let me finish this last spot." A moment later Adam put down his torch and walked over to the truck.

"Is everything okay?" he asked, apparently noticing the frustrated look on her face.

"Oh, yeah. Everything is just fine, other than this stupid dog won't get out of the truck."

"I thought I mentioned that she likes to go where you go."

"Likes to go with me? She doesn't even like me! Why would she want to go *with* me?"

"Well, when it comes down to it, you're pretty lucky that she even let you in the truck. Gordon always said that she thought it was hers, and that he was just the chauffeur. She always went with him pretty much wherever he went. He'd just leave the windows down during the summer so that it wouldn't get too hot."

"Come on. You want me to leave the windows down? What if someone comes and steals the truck."

A huge grin split Adam's face. "Seriously, city girl? To start with, we don't have much of a problem like that, at least in the small towns around here. Second, who in his right mind is going to reach into a vehicle that has a dog sitting watch on the front seat?"

Abby turned to look, and sure enough, Max was sitting proudly in the driver's seat of the pickup, watching the conversation out the windshield.

"Okay, I get it. But what if I don't want to take the fur ball with me? How do I get her out?"

"I would say you probably have a choice of accepting the situation, or buying another vehicle. She's a lot safer in the truck than chasing behind, and she'd probably take the house apart right now if you left her. Bella watches the place when Max isn't there, so it's safe. Max has lost a lot lately. It might just be time to go with the flow, so to speak."

Abby took a deep breath and looked back at Max who was still studying them through the windshield. "Okay. I guess she can come," she said grudgingly

Adam tried to cover a choke of laughter and disguise it as a cough, although he wasn't very successful.

Jaw tight, Abby continued, "She can come *this time,* but she'd better not eat the groceries on the way home."

"Oh, that's easy. If you get something you think she might be interested in, either put it in the bed of the truck, or when you leave the truck at the next spot, point at each bag and tell her 'this is no.'"

"No way."

"Sounds bizarre but it works. I've seen Gordon do it a hundred times. If you point to something and tell her that it's 'no' she won't touch it. Even if you're in the next place for hours, she won't touch it. Forget to tell her it's no, however, and all bets are off."

"Alrighty then," Abby said, getting back behind the steering wheel and looking at her copilot. "This is looking to become a more interesting trip than I imagined."

A little over forty-five minutes later Abby walked up to the sheriff's office in Rogers City. She opened the door and looked around the large room, eyes eventually resting on the tall, uniformed man sitting at the back.

"Deputy Morrison?"

"Yes." The man looked up from his paperwork. Blue eyes met hers, questioning.

Abby moved forward into the room as the man stood. She thrust her hand out. "I'm Abigail Williams. I called earlier about my uncle, Gordon Dorsey?"

"I'm pleased to meet you." Morrison said, nodding, face serious. "As I said on the phone, I'd be glad to talk with you, although I don't know what help I'll be." Morrison gestured toward his desk where an extra chair was waiting. "I pulled out the file and reviewed it, not that I don't remember most of what happened, but it looks like a pretty standard accidental death.

"We received a 911 call at six forty-two in the morning on the third of August from Adam Thomas, a tenant of your uncle's?"

Abby nodded her head.

"The report was that Mr. Dorsey was found floating close to the shore of Lake Ellen, in front of his home. It appeared that he'd fallen from the dock and hit his head. Mr. Thomas pulled him on shore and tried CPR, but had no success. He called 911, and fire department and sheriff's office responded. I was first on the scene, followed soon after by the ambulance and fire truck. They tried to revive Mr. Dorsey, but it was pretty obvious that he'd gone into the water quite a while before being discovered."

"Okay, but Rick Laskis, my uncle's lawyer, said that your office determined that he'd been drunk and fell. Knowing my uncle's past, I'm having trouble believing that story. And Adam, I mean Mr. Thomas, agrees with me and he knew my uncle better than any of us."

"There were several empty bottles on the deck which had contained..." Deputy Morrison looked down at the file in his hands. "...residue of what appeared to be home brewed cherry beer."

"What was his blood alcohol?" Abby queried. "Surely you tested that."

Deputy Morrison thumbed a few pages of paper, looking for a report, and frowned at what he read. "His blood alcohol was .02. Well within the legal limit, but he had been drinking, and there were three empty bottles on the deck."

"Why specifically do you think he just tripped, lost his balance and fell? He wasn't drunk. Did you question whether he might have been pushed?" Abby was getting frustrated with the answers she was getting.

"There was no indication that another person was there, Ms. Williams. From all reports your uncle was pretty well liked by the majority of people. There were no reports to indicate that he had any form of conflict with anyone." Deputy Morrison looked at Abby with sympathy in his blue eyes. "I'm sorry, but sometimes accidents happen."

"I'm sorry as well, Mr. Morrison. I just can't accept that right now. It just doesn't make sense." Abby looked down at her hands clasped in her lap. "Adam told me that there were a bunch of people who wanted my uncle's farm... developers who wanted to make it into a vacation spot. Maybe one of them did something to him."

"I'm afraid you're grasping at straws. Yes, the land is valuable. Your uncle owns all the land surrounding Lake Ellen. It's a small lake, sure, but split up the lakefront property and it would develop into a pretty penny. However, there's no way a developer would know that he'd be able to get the farm if your uncle were gone. This isn't a TV show or mystery novel, Ms. Williams. It's just an accident. I wish I could be of more help."

"Yeah, I wish you could too." Abby sighed then stood to go. "I hope you don't take offense though, if I ask around."

Deputy Morrison smiled at her with a sad look in his eyes. "Ms. Williams, I'm sure you're going to do exactly what you need to do to put this behind you. Feel free to call me if you come across something you think I should know, but I believe that you're going to find that we did a pretty thorough job of investigating the accident."

He held out a card for Abby to take. She looked at it quickly, noting that his first name was Benjamin as she slid the card into her purse, turned and headed out the door.

Once outside in the fresh air, she looked up and down the street. She needed more coffee, as well as some other staples. Adam had been diligently caring for her uncle's flourishing garden, so fresh produce wasn't an issue, and there was plenty of fish, beef and goat in the freezer, but some of the other basics were running low. In addition, the airline's restrictions on the size of items such as soap and shampoo meant that what she'd brought wouldn't last, especially if she planned on playing farmer much longer.

Adam told her that Rogers City had a grocery store, but she hadn't seen one upon arrival. Truth be told, however, she'd been so focused on trying to find the station, that she might have missed a small grocery store. After debating her options, Abby finally turned and headed back into the sheriff's station, where she found Deputy Morrison once again sitting at his desk, working on the stack of paperwork.

"Excuse me." Abby spoke, since the deputy hadn't reacted at the sound of the door.

Deputy Morrison looked up, then pushed back his chair and rose to his feet. "Yes, Ms. Williams, did you forget something?"

"No, well yes, actually. I need to pick up some groceries, and I have no idea where to find the store."

Smiling, Deputy Morrison approached the front of the office, snagging a folded brochure from a rack on the way past. He spread it out on the counter where Abby stood and she saw that it was a simplified map of the town - the type the chamber of commerce might put out for the tourists.

"The sheriff's station is right here." Morrison circled a small drawing of a brick building with a black pen. "And there's a Glenn's Grocery Store right here on the highway. They should have anything you need. Anything bigger, and you'll have to go into Alpena, or north to Cheboygan." He made another circle, then traced the route Abby would take to get to the store. He handed the brochure to Abby, who examined both the route and the brochure itself, noting the colorful map on one side, and the list of tourist attractions on the other.

An occupational hazard of working in advertising, she immediately noted things she would have done differently if she'd been in charge of designing the brochure. A slight smile twisted her lips. Maybe she should consider opening up shop. The farm had supported her uncle, well at least partially. Maybe it could support her until she got a business up and running.

A few minutes later Abby was back out on the street, studying the Dakota, and the furry occupant of the driver's seat who was examining her just as intently. Unfolding the brochure again, she estimated the distance to the grocery store Morrison indicated, debating whether it was at all possible to walk, at the same time telling herself that it would be silly to do so just to avoid driving under the watchful eye of Max, guardian of the Dodge. While she was standing there, studying the situation, Deputy Morrison opened the door, car keys in his hand.

"Is everything okay, Ms. Williams?" Morrison had a quizzical look in his bright blue eyes. He pulled a cap down over his sandy hair.

"Yes, thank you. I was just trying to decide whether to drive to the grocery store, or whether to go ahead and walk." Abby looked back at the truck and noticed that Max had disappeared from view at the arrival of the deputy.

"Seems like an easy enough question. It's over a mile. Why wouldn't you drive down there? Unless you're only planning on a couple of items, it doesn't make sense to walk."

"Yes, well," Abby said, "you don't have a critical co-pilot in your car either."

With a strange look on his face, Morrison turned and examined Abby's truck. "I don't see any..." Suddenly Max's head popped into view, causing the deputy to burst into laughter.

"I take it that this is your 'co-pilot'?"

"She most certainly is. I'd be careful calling her an 'it' if I were you. She might take offense and then who knows where you'll be. I've got this sneaking suspicion that we're dealing with a higher form of intelligence. Maybe an alien in a dog's body."

At Morrison's shocked look she quickly said, "I'm just kidding. Honest. It's just that she unnerves me. Every time she looks at me I feel like she's judging."

"I take it that she is your uncle's dog, and not yours."

"You've got that right, although as I'm informed, she's mine now. I just don't know if she realizes it yet."

"Now I remember Mr. Thomas saying he didn't know where Mr. Dorsey's dog was the morning of the accident; couldn't understand why she wasn't with him when he went into the water. I guess she turned up. She's sure a beauty. Australian Shepherd?"

"So I'm told." Abby smiled at Morrison, nodding as she opened the door to the truck. "I appreciate your time today deputy."

"No problem." He nodded at her and walked off toward an SUV with the Presque Isle Sheriff's Department logo emblazoned along the side.

Groceries stowed in the back of the truck, Abby headed back for the farm, praying that she'd be able to remember all the turns involved. She had just turned onto the final dirt road when the truck gave a little jig to the left, and she heard the unmistakable *whump, whump, whump* of a flat tire.

She pulled over to the side of the road and got out, looking at the driver's side tires. Sure enough, the front left tire was as flat as it could possibly be.

Great she thought. *What am I supposed to do now?* She looked at her cell phone, but there was no signal. Peering in the door at Max she said, "I don't suppose changing tires is one of those things that you know how to do, huh?"

Not even a woof dignified that question.

"I didn't think so," Abby grumbled.

Resigning herself to the inevitable, she walked around to the passenger side of the truck. Hoping beyond hope, she checked in the glove box, praying that her uncle had kept the manual for the truck in that location. She breathed a sigh of relief when she saw the fat book, and turned to the index, looking for the pages which specifically dealt with changing tires. There it was, toward the back, complete with instructions on how to free the necessary tools from under the back seat, and the spare from under the bed of the truck.

It wasn't long before she had the jack snug under the

front end of the truck, the rim cover off, and was trying to loosen the lug nuts on the tire itself. That's where the whole plan fell apart in Abby's estimation. The nuts refused to budge no matter how hard she pried at them.

"Seriously? Now what do I do?" Abby stood and looked around. Swamp on one side, forest on the other, ahead of her some large green fields with more forest, and behind her even more forest. She looked at her cell phone, hoping for a change in its condition. Still no bars appeared on the screen. Apparently in this particular hollow there was no service. Again.

"Okay, Max. I'm going to have to walk to get some help. You stay here and guard the truck, okay?"

Immediately Max jumped out the window and stood at Abby's side.

"I swear, if my uncle were here right now, he and I'd have a talk about dog training! Fine, you can come with me, but only if you behave yourself. Got it?"

Abby rolled up the windows of the truck and locked the doors. Adam might say that this was a safe area, but there was no point in being careless. Who knows, she thought, a delinquent deer might jump in and take off on a joy ride.

Abby and Max were only about a hundred feet down the road when she heard the crunch of wheels on gravel behind her. Turning, she saw a gunmetal gray truck liberally spattered with rust spots pulling up behind the Dakota. The door opened, and out stepped a tall man with dark brown hair, wearing a tan hooded sweatshirt, jeans and work boots. She waved at him, turned and headed back toward the truck.

"Hi, looks like you've got a problem here," the man called.

"Yeah. The tire gave up, and I can't seem to get the lug nuts off to change it." Abby approached the man, noticing the tan face and smile lines around his eyes.

He reached out his hand, and said, "My name is Jake Solinski. You must be Gordon's niece. Shame about what happened. Your uncle was a good guy."

"Does everyone around here know everyone else?" Abby laughed.

"I'm one of the neighbors. I own the farm down the road from his... I guess yours now." Jake frowned briefly. "As a matter of fact, it wasn't too hard to figure out who you were. You were driving Gordon's truck, and Max is with you. Hi Max."

Max approached Jake and allowed him to scratch her ears.

"Really! You let him touch you, but you won't let me anywhere near." Abby grumbled and Jake laughed at her expression.

"Takes some getting used to, doesn't it. I think it was two or three months before she would let me near her, and I used to see Gordon a lot. I've been trying to develop a CSA program, that's is a Community Supported Agriculture program. It will take a lot of us. The farmer's market is a start, but we can take it a lot farther, and Gordon was on board. He was helping me work with some of the others in the area. Hopefully we'll be able to keep it going even without him. Enough of that, however. Would you like some help getting that tire changed?"

"I thought you'd never ask." Abby said, smiling widely.

It didn't take long for Jake to solve the problem of the stuck lug nuts. Reaching into the toolbox at the back of the truck, he pulled out a four way lug wrench. Grinning at her he said, "These things make a world of difference. You get a little leverage, compared to those things they send with the trucks and cars when they're sold. You should never go anywhere without one of them. I'm surprised Gordon doesn't have one in the Dakota."

"To be honest, I think he might," said Abby, studying the tool in Jake's hand. "But I didn't realize what it was. I was just going off the instructions in the owner's manual."

"Ah, that explains it." Jake smiled at her, then turned back to the chore of changing the tire.

Popping the right end of the wrench onto the stuck lug nuts, he put his weight onto one of the cross bars, and with a screech, the nut came loose and began to spin easily. He repeated the action with the rest of the nuts, then finished jacking the truck off the ground so that he could pull off the tire.

"See, easy as pie," Jake joked with Abby. "Now just to get the tire out from under the truck, and for that we need these couple of long pieces. Screw them together, and thread them in by the license plate and into the slot. Then pray that the mud and salt hasn't corroded the mechanism to a degree that the tire won't start to drop."

"Is that possible?"

"Yeah, it's possible. But I doubt it knowing your uncle. He'd be pretty good about checking it out periodically, making sure there's air in the spare, and oiling the chain that the tire hangs on. And, if he didn't, Adam sure would."

Sure enough, the chain released smoothly, dropping the tire to the ground where Jake could grab it and drag it out. Shortly after that, with the flat tire thrown into the bed of the truck, Abby was ready to go.

"Make sure you take that tire in to get it fixed soon. You don't want to be driving around here without a spare," Jake said, smiling at her. "How long are you planning on staying?"

"I don't really know, right now. I've got a month off work. I had a lot of time accrued and I wasn't sure how much time I'd need to get everything taken care of here." Abby looked at the ground chewing her lip, trying to determine how much to tell Jake. She didn't know him, and if she truly believed that her uncle hadn't gone into the water on his own, then that meant that someone else had been there, and who knows who that someone could be.

Listen to me, she thought sarcastically, *just like all those mystery book heroines. Next thing you know I'll be facing down the killer and praying for some handsome guy to come to my rescue.* A bubble of laughter rose in her throat and bursting forth. She quickly converted it to a cough, although it must have sounded strange since Jake gave her a startled look..

"Well," he hesitated for a moment, and then continued. "If you decide to sell, I'd sure appreciate it if you'd let me know."

Abby looked at him, surprised.

"I'd sure hate to see that place turned into a vacation spot. See it split up and cabins surrounding the lake, people all over the place. I've seen it happen to other farms. City folk move in, then start complaining about the stink of fertilizer or of cows. They put a lot of pressure on the local governments, and soon the farmers are forced out."

"Was my uncle talking about selling?"

"He and I had talked a bit. There were a lot of people who wanted his farm. This is becoming a more popular place for down staters and that lake is a gold mine."

"My uncle didn't own the lake, though. Only the land around the lake." She and Rick had this discussion when Abby heard that her uncle's farm surrounded the lake entirely. Her initial reaction was *I own a frickin' lake!* Rick assured her that she didn't own a lake, no matter how small. Michigan law stated that an individual couldn't own navigable waters, and since the lake was joined to the Ocqueoc River by a narrow channel, it was considered navigable. But owning the land around the lake meant that while people could come in and fish, they couldn't get out of their boats without trespassing. For most it wasn't worth the effort to come up the Ocqueoc to the small lake, and Gordon had been left largely alone.

"He may not have owned the lake, but he could have split the land around the lake up into lake front property, put in a boat ramp and made a killing. He didn't want to see that happen, though." Jake looked her in the eyes. "And, you'd better believe that ticked a few people off."

Abby stared at Jake, open-mouthed. *Did he just tell me that my uncle was murdered?* She wondered frantically. *Maybe others have the same doubts that Adam and I have.*

"Do...," Abby started but Jake started talking like he hadn't heard her.

"It was nice meeting you, Abigail Williams. Your uncle was a great guy." Jake started walking back to his truck and opened the door to get in. "Don't forget to have that tire fixed. Say hi to Adam for me. I'm sure I'll be seeing you around."

Jake started the truck, and pulled away, waving at Abby as he left. Abby stood in the middle of the road wondering what had just happened. She looked at Max.

"That was sudden, wasn't it?"

Max just looked at her. Abby reached out her hand, and Max ducked away from the contact. "You mean it? We've just spent the morning together. You've sat in the truck next to me. Heck, you just let the neighbor, and a neighbor with a possible motive, mind you, scratch your ears, and I can't touch you?"

Frustrated, Abby opened the truck door and stood back for Max to jump in, then slid in herself, and headed for the farm.

Abby spent part of the afternoon getting familiar with her domain, even if it was a temporary kingdom, spending time out in the pasture, getting to know the animals. Unlike Max, Bella, the large Great Pyrenees that guarded the livestock, had no compunction about letting Abby pet her. The horses came up, nuzzling her pockets for treats, and the goats were anxious that they get their share of the attention.

Abby, who had been raised on the outskirts of the Phoenix Metropolitan area, hadn't had many animals of her own growing up, but she'd had friends who owned horses and goats, and had enjoyed going to their homes and playing with the animals. Since becoming an adult, however, while she'd occasionally felt the urge to get a dog or a cat, she always ended up deciding that her life was too hectic and too crazy to include a pet. It wouldn't be fair to the animal to be shut up all day, every day when she was at work. Someday, she told herself, someday, when she wasn't so driven, wasn't such a workaholic.

Abby took a deep breath, and headed back toward the house. While spending time outside with the animals was fun, dealing with the snarl of red tape that resulted when someone passed away was not. Regardless of how onerous it was, however, it needed to be dealt with, and sooner rather than later.

Several hour later Abby emerged from Gordon's office, brain whirling, feeling completely inadequate to the task of running the farm, and desperately seeking coffee. Or tea. Or cherry beer, whatever that was.

She'd managed to reach the proper authorities, chose a funeral home, and arrange for a memorial at the United Methodist Church in Millersburg. Gordon hadn't been much on attending church, but when he did go, that was his chosen destination. Gordon had specified cremation in his paperwork, so Abby arranged for that to take place immediately, even though the memorial was scheduled several weeks out so that she could get the word out to his friends.

Abby was pleasantly surprised to see that Rick had helped her uncle set up a family trust, placing all of his assets into that entity to keep it out of probate, making it much quicker and easier for Abby to take over the property. As Abby went through the collected mail from the past weeks, sorting the bills out from the trash, and making a list of companies to notify of her uncle's passing, she was struck by how simple he'd made his life. She was also struck by how accustomed she'd become to doing everything by computer. Gordon kept meticulous records of his expenses and income from the farm, and several other endeavors, but everything was in a huge ledger book, not on a computer spreadsheet.

Looking through Gordon's cabinets... *Damn, I've got to remember they're my cabinets now...* Abby eventually settled on an herbal tea, deciding that caffeine was not in her best interest if she wished to sleep well that night, but that it was too early for alcohol, even if in something that sounded as innocuous as cherry beer.

She stood at the kitchen window...*her kitchen window...* and stirred her tea, contemplating the view of the barn across the drive. Max was laying in the sun while Cali Cat seemed to be stalking her. In the pasture the cows and horses were apparently dozing in the late afternoon warmth. The goats weren't to be seen, but from what Adam said, no news was good news as far as they were concerned.

It was idyllic, and already she felt resentment at the short time she would have here, as well as frustration at the choices she had to make... whether to sell here and return to the heat and dust of Phoenix, or whether to roll the dice and try her luck in such a foreign setting.

She was startled out of her reverie by the ringing of the phone hanging on the wall over by the door. Only a few people knew she was at this phone number: Lucy, her boss, Rick and Deputy Morrison, and Adam of course. Anyone else trying to reach her would have tried her cell, which was only getting a signal on the top floor of the house, and not always even then. That morning, while in Rogers City, she'd checked and noted a number of missed calls and texts from Josh, all of which she'd dismissed. Her ex was one major check on the "stay in Michigan" side of the tally sheet.

She reached for the phone and looked for the caller ID. None there. Big surprise. She smothered an internal laugh. Her uncle must have been the leader of the Luddites from all the evidence of technology she could see on the place, although some of the equipment used in the trout operation seemed pretty up to date. She held the receiver to her ear, expecting to hear Lucy's girlish voice at the other end.

"Hello?" Nothing but silence met her greeting.

"Hello? Is anyone there? This is Abby Williams. Gordon Dorcy's niece..." thinking that maybe someone who hadn't heard of her uncle's death was trying to reach him and was surprised by the female voice answering the phone.

"Hi, Abby. It's me. Josh," A deep male voice finally answered. Josh. Ex-boyfriend, and current major complication in Abby's life. She was so shocked at the sound of his voice she was rendered momentarily speechless.

For three years of her life Abby and Josh Sanders had been together. During the last two years he'd moved into the apartment where she'd been living ever since graduating from college and moving back to Phoenix to work for Daniels Advertising.

However, Abby started noticing changes during the last year of their relationship. Josh had always been fun to be around. Abby had at times thought of him as a force of nature. Intense, full of energy and fun. Exciting. But in the final months that energy had become unfocused. He quite his job with one of the largest technology firms in the area, saying that the management was short-sighted. He decided to open his own consulting firm, working from their two bedroom apartment. He became increasingly jealous of Abby, suspecting her of being unfaithful, even as she was doing everything in her power to reassure him. Finally Abby couldn't take it any longer, and told him to leave. Even then it had taken an eviction notice and a sheriff's deputy to get him out of the apartment.

Abby changed the locks and told herself that this chapter of her life was over. Then the phone calls started. Josh begged Abby to take him back; threatened to hurt himself if she didn't, threatened to hurt her if she didn't. He called and texted incessantly, waited outside her apartment and office. Friends recommended she get a restraining order, but she just couldn't bring herself to take that last step. She kept telling herself he'd wear himself out, and he wasn't a real danger to her, or to himself, and that the restraining order was just a piece of paper and it would do nothing but keep the situation going even longer, and maybe even make it worse.

She sure as heck hadn't given him the phone number to her uncle's house, or even told him that she was leaving Phoenix for a month, and she was positive that no one else had told him either.

She momentarily considered slamming the phone back on its cradle, hesitated, then finally her curiosity and frustration got the better of her.

"Josh, why are you calling? How did you get this number? I told you I don't want to talk to you any longer. We're done. Move on." Abby spoke more harshly than she ever thought possible, feeling the growing tide of anger tighten her chest.

"Lucy gave it to me. I miss you, Abb. I thought maybe you'd reconsidered? We were good together for a while. I know I was a jerk, but I'm getting myself back together."

"There is no way in hell Lucy gave you this number. Dammit, Josh. Leave me alone. I haven't reconsidered. As a matter of fact, Josh, your call has just convinced me even more that we're done. I'm glad you're working on yourself, but we're not good together. Besides, I'm leaving Phoenix. Moving. It's over. We're over!"

"Abby, no! Where..."

"We're done!" Abby slammed the phone into its cradle and stood there trembling.

"Shit, shit, shit, shit, hell and damnation," Abby muttered to herself, trying to calm her racing heart. Why the hell had she told him she was moving? She couldn't move here. She'd been here fewer than two days and didn't know anything about running the farm. She slapped her open hand on the counter in frustration. The sting of her open palm focused her.

That's it. Everyone's right. I need to get a restraining order as soon as I get home. This crap has gotten way out of hand.

Finally under control, Abby picked up the phone again, and punched in the number for Lucy's cell. Typical of so many people these days, no one answered and the phone went to voice mail. Gritting her teeth, and wishing she could just send a text, Abby said, "Hey Luce, I just got a call from Josh. He said you'd given him this number. What gives? Give me a call back at this number, not my cell. There's like no signal here. I need to change carriers, I guess. Just call me ASAP."

Abby hung up the phone and wandered back over to the sink, where her cooling cup of tea sat forgotten. She picked it up and took a tentative sip. Gradually she felt her heart rate return to normal. Suddenly she started to cry. Too much had happened recently. Too damn much. She turned and sat down at the kitchen table, mug of tea in front of her, as tears streamed down her face unheeded, lost in a world of morose thoughts.

A short time later Abby became aware of the sound of an approaching vehicle from outside. A sudden cacophony of barks joined the sound of the engine, announcing the arrival of a guest. Rising to her feet, she reached for a dish towel, dampened it in the sink, and wiped her face. She glanced at the wall clock, and realized that it was nearly chore time.

Abby flipped off her sandals and picked up her sneakers, remembering what Adam told her that morning about the folly of wearing open-toed shoes around larger animals. Just as she was rising from the kitchen chair after tying the laces, she heard footsteps crunching in the gravel pathway, then a knock on the door.

"Hey Adam, come on in. No need to stand on ceremony," Abby called out. The door opened, but instead of Adam's cheerful, tanned face, she saw a stranger whom she guessed to be in his mid-50s, with silvered hair, wearing khakis, and a navy polo shirt with the logo of a real estate agency embroidered on the left breast. Max, apparently aggravated with this visitor but too well-mannered to bite him, pushed past his legs and came to stand next to Abby, eyes fixed intently on the man in the doorway.

"Ms. Abigail Williams?" The man approached Abby, hand held out.

Abby rose the rest of the way to her feet, and tentatively held out her hand. "Yes, I'm Abbigail Williams. Can I help you?"

"My name is Bill Sommerfield. I'm with Reliance Real Estate." Bill took Abby's hand and pumped it enthusiastically.

"I've been working with your uncle on developing his farm here. Damned shame about what happened. I was going by, and I thought I'd come in and introduce myself. Hopefully we can do business." Sommerfield fished in his pocket, and pulled out a glossy, embossed business card and held it out pinched between his index and middle fingers.

Abby felt like she'd been caught in a tornado. Sommerfield's words poured out in a torrent, the entire time the toothy grin never left his face. However, she noticed that it was a smile that never reached his eyes. Abby reached out and took the card, setting it on the table at her side.

"My uncle was selling the farm?"

An expression flitted across Sommerfield's face, so quickly that Abby almost missed it, and couldn't identify its meaning. The smile, if anything, grew even larger.

"We'd been talking about it for some time now," Sommerfield said. "That little lake of yours could be worth a lot of money. Down staters are always looking for lake front property, and even though Ellen isn't a large lake, it does connect with bigger lakes by a good, deep river. A little bit of work on the channel, and boaters would be able to zip right out to the larger bays." Sommerfield's fake smile got even broader, if that were possible, and Abby had a momentary concern that his face was going to split in half.

A mental shiver of distaste washed through her. He

was full of it. He was the epitome of the slimy salesman. *Well* Abby thought *two can play at that game* and she plastered a fake smile on her face.

"While I'm pleased to meet you, Mr. Sommerfield..."

"Please. Bill."

"Bill. While I'm pleased to meet you, I've only just found out that my uncle died, and that I inherited his farm. I have no idea about what I'm going to do with it, and I plan on talking with a lot of the people who knew my uncle, and his operation."

The smile on Sommerfield's face flickered briefly, but Abby continued on as though she'd missed that small tell.

"I've already had at least one offer. One that would keep the land a farm which I imagine is what my uncle would prefer." Abby felt justified in exaggerating Jake Solinski's comment slightly. "But I appreciate your interest, and should I decide to sell the farm for development, I'll give you a call." Sommerfield's smile which had faded at the mention of another offer, started to grow again until Abby dropped her next line.

"Since I don't know anyone around here, I'm sure I'll be talking with a number of real estate agents and developers before I make my decision, but your name will be at the top of the list."

Direct hit. The smile fled Sommerfield's face altogether, and storm clouds seemed to build in his steel gray eyes.

"I appreciate your wanting to be careful, Abby. However, I have done a lot of the groundwork for development. You'll make nowhere near the money if you sell it as a farm, and the odds are the new owner will sell and make the profit. The way I see it, you owe me." Sommerfield's voice had taken on a harsher note.

"I owe you?" Abby stopped in her tracks, staring at Sommerfield. "From what I'm told, my uncle never intended to sell for development. I owe you nothing." *So much for diplomacy,* Abby thought.

Sommerfield began to sputter but Abby wasn't finished. "Unless Uncle Gordon had a signed contract with you, giving you exclusive rights to represent the family trust...." Abby paused for a second, giving Sommerfield time to respond, but with an inward fish pump, sure that her uncle would never work with a jackass like Sommerfield. "Unless you can show me that piece of paper, then you have no further business with me, or my uncle's estate." Abby continued, "Now, I'm sorry to hurry you, but I believe I see Adam's truck coming up the drive. It must be time for chores."

Abby moved to encourage Sommerfield out the door, ignoring the poorly concealed look of fury on his face. Max, glued to Abby's side for the duration of the confrontation, moved forward with her which appeared to be the deciding factor in Sommerfield's decision to retreat. Adam's old red Ford truck had crunched to a stop outside the barn, and she could see Adam himself standing next to the vehicle, looking toward the open door of the house as Sommerfield and Abby emerged. Adam started to move slowly around the bed of the truck, heading toward the duo, a wary look on his face.

"Abby, is everything okay?" Adam asked, eyeing Sommerfield, dislike obvious in his expression.

"Yeah, I think so. Do you know Bill Sommerfield, Adam?"

"We've met." Adam nodded abruptly in Sommerfield's direction.

Abby turned her attention back to the real estate agent. "Mr. Sommerfield, I appreciate your stopping by to introduce yourself, but I doubt we'll have further cause to run into one another." Abby turned on her heel, and moved off, pulling Adam and Max with her. "I'm guessing it's chore time, Adam?"

Abby refused to look back at Sommerfield, standing next to his car, but instead moved resolutely toward the open barn doors. Adam looked momentarily uncertain, then moved off after Abby and Max. Abby heard the low rumble of Sommerfield's SUV as it started, and the grinding of the tires on gravel as he headed off down the driveway toward the county road.

Abby blew out a breath she didn't know she'd been holding, and turned to Adam who was studying her intently, a frown creasing his forehead.

"What was that all about?"

A brief laugh blew out of her lungs. "Bill was telling me that he and Gordon had been working together to sell the farm for development."

A look of outrage replaced the frown on Adam's face.

"There is no way on God's green earth or hell's half acre that Gordon would work with that slimy asshole."

"No, I don't think so either. I think he was hoping that he could sort of get his foot in the door while the heir was uncertain about what was going on, convince me that the two of them were in business together in the hopes that I'd agree to develop, or sell for development."

Adam shook his head disgustedly, and his right hand scrubbed through his close-cropped dark hair. "Yeah, I'm sure you're right. He's been after Gordon for awhile, but your uncle shut him down pretty quickly every time. There's no way he wanted to develop the farm. He..." Adam noticed that Abby had become distracted and was no longer paying close attention to what Adam was saying.

"Abby?"

"Yeah? Oh, I'm sorry Adam. You don't think, do you, that Sommerfield might have done something to maybe get my uncle out of the way? I mean if Uncle Gordon was refusing to do business with him, Sommerfield might have thought that there were no heirs, or that any heirs there were wouldn't be interested in becoming fish farmers and would be thrilled to accept a large wad of cash to have the whole thing taken off their hands."

Adam came to an immediate stop in front of the barn, reached out and grabbed Abby's arm to spin her toward him. Her attention came back into focus, looking into Adam's shocked dark brown eyes.

"You don't really think that Bill Sommerfield would have killed your uncle over a land development deal do you?"

"I don't know, Adam, but from the way Sommerfield was talking, there was a lot of money at stake, both for Gordon, and for the developer." Abby blew out another breath, causing her bangs to dance on the breeze. "Hell, you know Sommerfield better than I do. You know everyone around here better than I do and you probably know more about the amount of money involved in this type of deal. What do you think? Bill "shark's grin" Sommerfield seemed pretty sketchy to me. Do you think he's the type?"

Adam's look of shock dissolved into one of concentration as he contemplated Abby's questions. Finally after a lengthy internal debate that Abby watched play out on his face, Adam took a deep breath, and his eyes met hers.

"I really don't know, Abby. Yeah, it's a lot of money involved. I've known farmers who have retired well because they had some desirable land and sold it for development. Your property surrounding Lake Ellen is probably more in demand than any of those places.

"Bill Sommerfield is pretty slimy, and he was riding your uncle pretty hard, but he wouldn't have had any idea who would inherit if Gordon was killed. For all Sommerfield knew, Gordon might have left it to me, specified in the trust that it only be sold as farm land, or donated it to some Wounded Warriors type of organization. There were a couple of us who knew about you, but none of us would have said anything to Slimy Sommerfield. He'd have been taking a big chance killing off Gordon in the hopes that the heirs would sign with him in a development deal."

Abby felt the momentary thrill caused by her certainty that she was hot on the trail of her uncle's killer dissolve into more frustration as Adam pointed out the flaws in her hypothesis.

"Yeah, Morrison said something along those lines as well. I still think it's worth checking out," Abby said stubbornly. "You and I both know that Gordon didn't die the way they said he did. Someone must have killed him."

"How do you propose to 'check him out'?" Adam looked at Abby quizzically.

"I don't know." A look of intense concentration settled on her face. "But I know from talking to Deputy Morrison that the police aren't looking past the surface of the matter. If anyone is going to find out the answers, it's going to have to be me."

10

Consciousness came with the dawn's light. Warm dog breath stirred Abby's bangs and made her wrinkle her nose. Cautiously she opened her left eye a mere slit then closed it again, willing Max to give up and leave the room. Mentally she promised God anything He wanted, as long as He'd take the damned dog away.

The way she saw it, God was laughing at her since the subject of her fervent prayers saw fit at that moment to sneeze in her face.

"Max!" Abby jerked back, both eyes open now, glaring at the black, tan and white face at the edge of the bed, mouth open and tongue lolling, as though Max were laughing at her.

"Don't suppose I could talk you into another half hour or so, could I?"

Max replied with a soft woof, followed by the now familiar yodeling sounds that seemed so much like speech.

"Maybe fifteen minutes? I'll make you scrambled eggs and cheese for breakfast."

Max snorted, spun and headed out of the bedroom. Upon realizing that Abby was not immediately jumping out of bed to follow, she turned back and uttered a sharp bark, which Abby took to mean that Max could not be bribed any more than God could, and that Abby better get her butt in gear.

She groaned, shifting herself deeper into the nest of blankets, only to feel a sharp stabbing pain in her left foot.

Abby shot upright, staring at the bottom of the bed where the second member of the wake up tag team was stalking Abby's feet under the covers. Just as Abby opened her mouth to protest, the cat pounced again, grabbing the lump that was Abby's right foot in her claws and gnawing on the big toe.

"Hey!" Abby squeaked, jerking both feet back underneath her, leaving the cat the undisputed queen of the foot of the bed. "That was my foot! Not some mouse for you to catch!"

Cali Cat sat looking at her, tail lashing, obviously prepared to continue the game as she saw fit.

Finally resigned to the fact that she was outnumbered, and badly outmatched, Abby threw the blanket back and swung her legs out of bed. She scrubbed her face with her hands, trying to force wakefulness into her brain. Lucy had called late the night before, apologizing for forgetting the three hour time difference caused by daylight savings time.

Just as Abby had supposed, Lucy said she hadn't even talked to Josh and was infuriated that he'd said that she'd been the one to give him the phone number to the cabin in Michigan. Lucy promised to investigate at her end to try and determine who had leaked the information.

With that, the two slid easily into discussion about what was happening both in the northeast and the southwest. Even though she'd only been gone for two days, Abby felt as though she was years away from Phoenix and the big city life, while on the other hand Lucy was mesmerized by Abby's description of the farm and its location.

"You mean you have to go over an hour to the nearest big city?"

"You make it sound as though I have to get on a rocket and take a six month voyage to another planet."

Lucy's tinkling laugh came over the phone and Abby could picture the petite brunette as clearly as if she were sitting across the table. "It seems that way. I didn't really think there was anywhere in the United States that was farther than five minutes away from a McDonalds or a Walmart."

"Both can be had only an hour away, my friend," Abby chuckled. "I'm sure there are other places where you'd have to drive even farther, although I can't think of them off hand. However, for some of our favorite restaurants, I'm told we're out of luck."

"Better learn to cook then, Abby. I'm guessing Domino's doesn't deliver out there."

"I'm pretty sure no one delivers out here! But, what do you mean I have to 'learn to cook!' I know how to cook, thank you very much! Besides, I don't think that Max will criticize the cuisine."

There was a momentary silence over the line, then, "Oooh, two days out there, and there's already a Max. Tell me about him."

"A lot of hair, golden brown eyes..." Abby grinned to herself, picturing the look on Lucy's face.

"Sounds good so far," Lucy said encouragingly.

"And female."

"What!" Lucy screeched.

"And canine."

Lucy started laughing so hard she choked, causing Abby to call her name several times into the phone receiver.

"Lucy! Luce, are you okay?"

"Yeah. You rat! You could have led off with that! Here I was thinking that you'd found a handsome farmer type, and I was going to lose you to the enticements of northern Michigan."

Abby grinned. "No, at least not yet, although this place is growing on me. Max is Uncle Gordon's Australian Shepherd. She apparently owns the place, and I'm just the one who pays the bills... or who will pay the bills."

"You know, Abby, you're sounding like this place has gotten its hooks into you."

"It is a beautiful area." Abby could feel herself drifting off mentally and administered a shake, metaphorically speaking. "Now, what's happening in the office?"

For the next hour and a half the two talked about all the things that had happened in the past few days. Finally, Abby noticed that the wall clock was reading 12:30. *No wonder she was so exhausted.*

Yawing so widely that she thought her jaw would crack apart, Abby told Lucy that she had to get some sleep before the Max/Cali Cat wake up duo appeared at her bedside in the morning. She hung up the receiver and stumbled up the stairs to the bedroom, where she fell asleep to the sound of loons on the lake outside.

Twenty minutes later found Abby showered and seated at the kitchen table, clutching a steaming cup of caffeine when Adam knocked on the door, then opened it and stepped in without waiting for Abby to call out.

"Morning, Adam. Want some high octane coffee?" Abby gestured toward the coffee maker sitting on the counter next to the sink.

"Sure." Adam opened the correct cabinet, locating a large mug, reminding Abby again that Adam was so much more a part of her uncle's life than she ever was, yet she was the one to inherit the farm. A small frisson of discomfort shivered its way down her back. *Not Adam. He wouldn't.* Abby resolutely pushed the thought down, stomping it into submission mentally.

As Adam poured the coffee, he looked back over toward Abby. "You look fried, Abby. Trouble sleeping last night?"

"Late phone call from a friend in Phoenix." Abby hesitated, undecided about how much to tell Adam about the reason for Lucy's call. While she'd only known Adam two days, and was positive he wasn't involved in Gordon's death (again that small twinge of doubt), she still wasn't sure that their budding friendship was to the point where she wanted to talk to him about Josh, ex-boyfriend and apparent psycho stalker. Finally deciding that this little tidbit could wait for a later time, Abby took another sip of her wake up juice, and asked, "What's the plan for the day?"

"Well, The Beaches restaurant called, and they would like some trout for their Friday fish special, and we've got the farmer's market tomorrow. So, we're going to be processing some fish today."

Abby stopped in mid sip as Adam was talking, then, suddenly realizing that her lips were burning, she jerked the mug away from her mouth, and started coughing. Setting the coffee on the table and wiping her mouth, eyes streaming, Abby looked up at Adam who was watching with a grin on his face.

"By processing you mean...?"

"By processing I mean we have to catch the fish, dispatch them humanely, clean them, and get them on ice, ready to deliver." Adam's tone was excessively formal, his expression bland, but Abby could see the laugh in his dark eyes.

"That's what I thought you meant," Abby said glumly.

"It's not that bad," Adam smiled sympathetically.

"Say the fish?"

"It's a *fish* farm, Abby." Adam sounded exasperated, as though this topic had come up before. "Cows are butchered, so are sheep and pigs, and I sure don't see you turning away from your bacon or your hamburgers."

"Yeah, but I'm not the one ending their lives."

"No, you're the one that their lives are being ended for. Face it, if no one ate beef, or lamb, or pork, then none of these animals would be raised for food. The fish are no different, but we try to do it in the least stressful way, least painful way possible."

Abby took a deep breath, picked up her coffee and took another drink. Then she pushed the chair back, and stood, turning to set her mug in the kitchen sink. Reaching up, she bunched her light brown hair and slid the elastic from around her wrist and twisted it twice creating a thick ponytail.

"Well, okay then. Let's get the chores done, then catch some fish. No guts no glory." She headed out the back door without looking over her shoulder to see if Adam was following, but a groan told her he was back there somewhere and didn't appreciate the pun.

The two of them headed across the barnyard, Max running ahead and disappearing into the open double doors. Abby once again felt a growing sense of awe that she now owned something so beautiful, so peaceful, and so very different from Phoenix. Greens like this didn't exist there. She never imagined that they existed anywhere. She also became even more strongly aware of a sinking feeling at the thought of leaving in a few weeks, even if she kept the property and returned for vacations. This was hers. It felt more right than anything she had ever felt before.

"Hey Abby, are you coming?"

Without realizing it, Abby had come to a stop and was just staring witlessly at the barn.

"Sorry, Adam, right with you." She picked up her pace and caught up quickly.

"By the way, my mother is coming Sunday evening, and was wondering if you'd like to come over for dinner." There was a tone in Adam's voice that was hard to interpret.

"Yeah, that sounds great. Does your mother live close by?

Adam nodded. "Well, sort of close by. She and Dad had a place outside Ossineke south of Alpena. It's not too bad a drive, and I think she's been lonely since Dad died a few years ago, so she usually runs over once a week or so."

"That's great, I guess." Abby glanced over at Adam from the corner of her eye, curious about the wry note in his voice. His expression said that said maybe it wasn't as great as all that.

"Well, I'm glad to see her and all, but she hasn't been all that happy since Jenn moved in... Jenn says that Mom doesn't think she's good enough for me. I also think Mom took Gordon's death pretty hard."

"They knew each other?" Abby asked, then answered her own question. "Of course they knew each other. She'd want to know the man who was helping you out."

"Yeah, it began that way." Adam smiled sadly. "I think though that she'd started to look at Gordon as a possible new husband. She was always bringing him things she'd baked, or offering to do mending, clean the house or do other things for him. Drove him up a tree. Max can't stand her, especially since Gordon's death." Adam's expression became if anything, even more morose. "I feel bad for her. I mean I love her. She's my mother. But she can be a bit... well a little... overwhelming and controlling."

"Don't worry. I'd love to meet her. What time do you want me over there, and can I bring anything with me?"

Adam's expression lightened and he smiled over at Abby. "If we start chores, or make that you start chores," he looked at Abby with a mischievous smirk on his face, "at five or thereabouts, they'll be done by six or so. Say we eat at six-thirty? And, no, don't bring anything. She'll have half the grocery store with her."

Abby grinned up at Adam. "I'll be there. Sounds like fun."

With that, the two headed into the barn and started the now familiar routine of making sure all the animals had their feed, and the goat was milked. Abby was proud to note that she seldom needed to ask Adam what needed to be done next, and that Autumn, the large brown and white milk goat, only kicked over the bucket twice. She may have only been there for two days, but Abby was beginning to believe that her uncle was right, and that she had the potential to make this a way of life. Her way of life. A warm euphoric feeling of peace floated down over Abby, and she was afraid that a sappy smile was planted on her face.

Then she was introduced to the fish house.

No euphoria, no matter how embracing could stand up to the fish house.

When the morning chores were finished, and with buckets of fish food in hand, the two of them headed up the path for the string of ponds.

"I figure we'll process about a hundred twenty trout today," Adam said, barely breathing hard from the climb.

"How... long will it take?" Abby gulped at the air, convinced that there wasn't enough oxygen in the world to satisfy her body.

"I figure we can get it done in a few hours... maybe half a day since you'll be slow at first. The Beaches' chef, Raymond Davidson, likes the fish to be very fresh, so when they order, I like to get it done on Thursdays, and deliver first thing Friday morning. I've kept up with the orders, but not the farmer's market since Gordon's... accident." Abby could hear an almost physical wince in his voice when he talked about her uncle's death. Unaware that Abby had picked up on his discomfort, Adam continued.

"I wasn't sure what to do afterward, you know. I mean the daily chores have to be done, but I wasn't sure about processing the fish, and I didn't want to get accused of taking money from the estate, but Rick said to try and keep the business running the same as usual until Gordon's heir had been contacted. There is at least one other trout farm in the area which would love to slide into the restaurants we supply."

The two of them reached the lowest and the largest of the ponds and set down the buckets of fish pellets.

"The farmer's market was too much for me, though. With the restaurants I could deliver the fish, and come back out to the shop, whereas with the farmer's market you've got to be there at the booth either one or two days, and my business needed to be taken care of too."

"It's fine, Adam. I just really appreciate all you've done keeping the farm going so well until things got straightened out. I know it couldn't have been easy."

Adam gave Abby a wry smile, sadness lurking in his eyes. "It's the least I could do for Gordon, and I love the farm almost as much as he did, I think. There was no way I was going to let it crash and burn."

"Adam...," Abby paused, unsure of how to ask the question that had been plaguing her since she met both he and Jenn. "Why did my uncle leave the farm to me?" From everything she'd heard, it seemed as though Adam was almost like a son to Gordon. It had to have stung that the farm he loved so much was going to someone who had no idea how to run it.

Adam started to head toward a shed set back in the trees that Abby hadn't really noticed before. "You're his only relative. I may love the farm, but you're his niece. Family comes first." Adam tipped the padlock on the door toward him, and Abby could see him insert the small brass key and turn it.

"Rick Laskis said that Uncle Gordon thought I had "potential," whatever that meant."

Adam gave the lock a push, and Abby could hear it click open.

"There's that too." Adam looked back over his shoulder to where Abby was standing with the buckets and gave her a grin, all clouds blown away. "He was sure that in that citified body lurked a secret country girl. You made a heck of an impact on him when you were younger."

"You've got to be kidding!" Abby snorted. "I was this gangly, rebellious teenager, and I only saw him for a short time before he eventually left. I do remember he and I went hiking up in the mountains after he got back from his tour of duty and was released from the hospital. He said it was part of his rehabilitation, you know, from losing his leg. I never wanted to come back home it was so beautiful. He seemed so sad when he came back from the Middle East, but out in the mountains, or on the lake he was different. It was like weights lifted off him and he was free..." Abby's voice trailed off as she remembered that short period with her uncle, and regretted not making more of an effort to spend time with him after she became an adult.

Adam turned to face her. "All I can say, Abby, is that your uncle thought you belonged here, and that you would love it as much as he did. I think he was probably right. Now, come help me with these coolers." Adam reached inside the door of the shed and pulled out two white, industrial sized (or as Abby thought, "bus sized") coolers, sliding one toward her, and grabbing the other by the handles on the side

Abby approached the shed, and peered in as she picked up her cooler. From the outside it was just an average gambrel roofed shed, with weathered gray siding. It was larger than most, but nothing out of the ordinary. She hadn't paid much attention to it before, just thinking it contained equipment necessary for maintaining the ponds if anything.

Instead, and in spite of the dark interior, she could tell it was floored with pristine white linoleum, and the walls had been finished and painted a light color, probably white. At the far side of what appeared to be a twenty-foot space stood an industrial sized ice machine, humming quietly in the dim light and next to it a large stainless steel cooler.

Adam, having apparently noticed her preoccupation with the shed, set down his cooler and returned. He reached inside to the right of the door and flipped on a bank of overhead florescent shop lights so Abby could see the big double stainless steel sink along the right hand wall with an expanse of stainless counter stretching out from the right side.

Although everything was spotless, the interior of the shed held the unmistakable olfactory residue of the past fishy visitors.

"Why build this up here?" Abby asked as she stepped into the building, shivering slightly as she looked at the knives lined up on the silver gray counter. "Why not just use the kitchen, or build it down closer to the barn."

"Because we're selling the fish through the restaurants and farmer's market we have to maintain a facility that meets the state's requirements. Gordon said he preferred to have things up here close to the ponds. He said there was no point in hauling everything down the hill. We harvest and clean them up here, then refrigerate them until we take them into town on ice in the big coolers. We'll load the coolers in the big wagon in the barn and haul them down to the Dakota to load them."

"Wait a minute! Wagon?" Abby looked at Adam aghast. "You mean there's a wagon down there, and I just finished hauling these buckets up the hill. I've hauled buckets up the hill for the past two days?"

Adam laughed at her appalled expression. "Yeah, there's a metal wagon that fits a bale of hay. Gordon always said it was harder to haul up the hill loaded and not tip over than it was to carry up the buckets by hand. I don't know whether he was right or wrong, we just always did it this way."

Abby studied the shed again. "Maybe he built the fish house up here because he didn't like having the fish ghosts near the house," she teased. If the gloomy interior of the fish house wasn't haunted by the dearly departed trout, it certainly should be. Although everything was pristine, the shed maintained a pervasive air of... sadness if that made any sense, which Abby thought it probably didn't.

"Have you guys ever thought of putting in a window or four? Maybe brightening the place up?"

"Well, we thought of it, but we really didn't spend that much time in here. It's a very small operation and Gordon really only sold the excess fish, beyond what he needed for himself. I imagine though, we would have added windows if he'd ever come across any salvage ones."

"Well, I can tell you right now, if I stay, we're getting windows! Now, let's get on with this. What do we do next?"

Adam handed Abby a pair of waders, and a large net, and taking the coolers and a long rolled bundle, they headed the short distance to the edge of the pond where the oldest fish resided.

"It takes a year to fourteen months before a trout is ready to harvest. Generally we're looking for ones that are between one and a quarter to one and a half pounds in weight." Adam stepped gingerly into the pond, feeling for the gravel bottom, then gesturing for Abby to follow.

"Because we generally don't process that many fish, we just push them to the far side of the pond, then net them and put them in the holding pen over there."

Abby looked in the direction that Adam pointed, and noticed that there was a small area staked out in the pond. She hadn't paid much attention to it before, but could now see that some type of loosely woven material was stretched from stake to stake, creating a fully enclosed square. The loose weave of the barriers allowed water to pass through, making it perfect to hold the fish after they were caught, if only for a short time.

"How do we get the trout to all go to that end of the pond so we can net them? I'm guessing they're not putting up their fins and volunteering."

"We'll push them there using the long net." Adam handed her the edge of the large rolled bundle, and showed her how to stretch it out until it developed into a large flat net on floats. They each took an edge, and Adam showed her where to walk, pulling the net behind her. Weights on the lower edge of the net caused it to drag on the bottom of the pond behind her. With Adam doing the same at the other end of the net, the fish would be confined into an ever decreasing space.

"Just move slowly and steadily toward the end of the pond that has the holding pen. You want to be calm and slow to avoid stressing the fish. They're really not all that difficult to catch when they're confined to the smaller area."

The two started, Abby dragging her edge of the net behind her, moving in the direction that Adam indicated. At the other side of the pond Adam did the same.

Abby noticed a flash of movement in the water, and looked back toward the middle of the pond.

"Adam, some of the fish have escaped." Abby was sure that she was doing something wrong.

"Don't worry. Some always make it through. Either they're too small, in which case we don't want them this time anyway, or they manage to get by some other way. It doesn't matter much since we've got more than enough corralled for what we need." He gestured at the teeming scaled hoard now crowded together.

Once the fish were concentrated into less than half the pond, Adam showed Abby how to wade out, and quickly scoop the trout out of the writhing mass of fish swarming around her legs. Once he got one in the net, he deposited it in what he called a "grading" box, and if it was the size he wanted, he released it into the small holding pen. If it was too small, he'd flip it back out into the far side of the pond to go free.

It didn't take the two of them long to gather 120 fish into the small holding area, and Abby found she was thoroughly enjoying herself wading around in the water, splashed by the thrashing of the fish, and the splattering droplets off the wet net. It had turned into a warm day and the touch of water was refreshing.

She looked briefly over toward the lake, thinking that maybe when all of this was done she'd treat herself to a swim. Then she remembered that Gordon had drowned in that sparkling green water, and the pleasant anticipation soured slightly.

"Okay, Abby, now the fun stuff is over." Adam pulled Abby's attention back to the job at hand. She cringed, knowing what came next, if not exactly how it was going to happen. She'd found she enjoyed watching those darting shadows in the water, looked forward to seeing the fish rush for the food that she brought, and the idea of killing some of them caused her stomach to twist.

Adam demonstrated how to quickly dispatch a fish in a method called pithing, the way a chef dispatched a lobster before tossing it in the boiling water. Adam explained that it wasn't that common in commercial operations, as it took a little longer, and a lot more expertise, but that Gordon felt it was the least painful, most humane way to achieve his goal. Since her uncle processed relatively few fish, he could afford to do it in any way he wished.

Before long, Adam and Abby had two full coolers of glistening trout ready to be cleaned. Each taking a handle, they carried first one, then the other container up to the fish house, and the real work began.

"Trout bones are very fine and their scales are tiny, so all we need to do is clean them and then pack them in ice," Adam explained as he showed her how to remove the entrails thoroughly and then wash out the body cavity. "We leave the head and tail on and just send them this way. With a lot of other fish, like bass, you have to remove the large scales, and probably fillet them to get rid of the bones. That's not needed with the trout. It's one of the reasons your uncle liked raising them.

"If a restaurant wants fillets, we can accommodate them, but The Beaches' specialty is whole baked trout with citrus, so we don't need to bother. It goes a lot faster that way."

Abby nodded, as she bent over her fish, trying to get the knife at the right angle and not remove a few of her fingers in the process. She chewed on her lower lip in concentration.

"How's it going?" Adam looked over her shoulder at her handiwork.

"Well, I've got a long way to go if I'm going to become a serial killer, but I'm getting better."

"You'll get the hang of it." Adam grinned at her look of discomfort.

"Did you struggle with it?" Abby asked, and then kicked herself mentally. He grew up around here. He probably learned how to clean a fish before he could write his own name.

"Nah, not really. I was brought up hunting and fishing," Adam said, confirming Abby's suspicions. "Besides, your uncle said that you should always give thanks when taking the life of something for food. Doing that sort of changes the perspective a bit. We're all part of the circle of life after all."

"If you start singing songs from the *Lion King* to me, I swear I will hit you with this fish," Abby grumbled good-naturedly.

A few hours later there were a 120 fresh trout in the cooler, Abby's shoulders ached, and the fish house had garnered a new crop of trouty ghosts, if there were such a thing. Briefly Abby threw out a mental thanks for those who gave their lives, figuring it couldn't hurt. Maybe the 'attitude of gratitude' would keep her dreams from being filled with trout bearing knives tonight.

After returning the stainless steel surfaces of the fish house back to their previous gleaming condition, the two stepped outside and Adam turned and snapped the padlock shut with a click.

"Why lock this door when practically nothing else on the place is ever locked?" Abby asked. She was still trying to get used to the idea that she didn't need to lock the door of the house whenever she walked outside, and the barn was open most of the time from what she could tell.

"We had some problems with people sneaking in and stealing fish a few years back. They'd hike through the woods and use the nets in the shed to catch what they wanted, then hike back out. So, Gordon decided he would be better off locking the nets up. It's not that uncommon for someone to be hiking with a backpack, even though the land is posted. However, it would be a dead giveaway for someone to be caught with a six foot net hiking through the woods, not to mention damned difficult where the undergrowth is thicker." Adam gestured toward the heavy wall of trees and bushes rimming the top of the hill above the topmost pond.

Suddenly Max, who had been lying outside the fish house while the two humans worked inside, took off toward the upper ponds like she was shot out of a cannon. Abby's mouth dropped as she watched with shocked eyes, thinking the dog had finally lost her mind once and for all.

"What the..."

Adam laughed at her expression. "Watch." Just as he said that, a large blue gray bird with impossibly long legs leaped into flight as Max skidded to a stop, barking, at the edge of the second pond.

"Max helps Bella keep an eye on the livestock, and the fish are part of the livestock. We hang that shade cloth to help keep out the eagles and the herons, like that one, but sometimes they get in anyway."

"Why don't you want the eagles and the herons here? That one is absolutely beautiful." Abby watched the huge bird disappear down toward the lake where she lost sight of it in the trees.

"They eat fish. Fish that make us money and feed us. And they can eat a lot. Gordon said that the first year he set things up, before he hung the cloth, and before Max and Bella came, the eagles and the herons wiped out most of a pond of juveniles."

Abby had learned the day before that Gordon didn't hatch his own fish, but instead ordered small "fingerlings" from a hatchery down state. Adam had told her Gordon had no desire to set up an entire hatchery system, so instead he just periodically ordered a tanker of fingerlings, or trout which were two to five inches long, and feeding on their own. These young fish went into the top pond. Then as they grew, and hit certain size milestones, they were moved down into the next lower pond, then the next, until they wound up in the large pond, ready to harvest. Considering that it took over a year for the fish to matriculate through the several ponds, she could see how a couple of ravenous large birds devouring most of a crop, could cause major problems in the cash flow later on.

With the fish house cleaned and all the equipment packed safely away, Adam and Abby headed back down the hill in companionable silence. Feeling a few rumbles of hunger, she looked at her watch and was surprised to see it was after 1:00 in the afternoon.

"Hey Adam, do you want some lunch? I'm starving."

"Thanks, I'd like to, but I've got to head for Gorski's farm over by Posen. They've got a tractor that's broken down, and I told them I'd come up this afternoon to get it up and running. He's got a couple of fields of potatoes he needs to get gathered, and I wouldn't want to hold him up any longer. There's a lot of rain predicted for the beginning of next week."

"What fun you have," Abby said, grinning in his direction. "Are you going to be back in time for chores? I'm not sure I'm ready to solo."

"Yeah, there shouldn't be a problem. If I'm late I'll give you a call and let you know. You'd be able to start on your own at least, and I could check when I got back." Adam smiled at the dubious look on her face. "I think you'll be surprised at how much you remember. Besides, I'm sure if you forget to feed someone, then that someone would let you know in no uncertain terms."

Abby could picture a mass prison break if she dropped the ball in regards to feeding the goats and grimaced. "You might be right, but I'd still feel better if you stopped by to make sure Max hasn't locked me in the barn and staged a coup. What..." Abby noticed a shocked look on Adam's face at her comment.

"I forgot about this until you said 'locked in the barn,' but Max was missing the morning I found Gordon, which is weird since Max was never far from Gordon's side. With everything happening so fast, I didn't really notice that she was gone until just before the sheriff's deputy was getting ready to leave."

"Deputy Morrison mentioned that you were concerned about where Max was. Where did you finally find her?"

"She was locked in the fish house raising holy hell, but I couldn't hear her down by the lake. It may not look like much, but the fish house is well insulated."

Abby looked at Adam confused. "I thought you kept

it locked all the time. How on earth could she have gotten locked in?"

"That's the strange thing. It was locked. I thought maybe she'd gone in there with Gordon the evening before when he was taking care of the fish. We have to check the pH level of the water frequently, and the equipment is kept in a cabinet in there. Max isn't supposed to go into the shed, but I thought maybe there was a mouse or something that she'd chased in while Gordon was out at the pond, and then he shut and locked the door without realizing she was there. That in and of itself would be strange, since he said he just didn't feel right when she wasn't nearby. It was almost like she was an extra limb. But now..." Adam's voice trailed off and he stood with a faraway look in his eyes, concentrating on a memory that Abby couldn't see.

"But now...?" Abby encouraged Adam to continue.

"Well, if you're right, and someone killed Gordon, that person must have locked Max into the fish house."

"That means that she knew the person, doesn't it?" Abby thought about the implications of Max being lured away from Gordon and locked into a space which was supposed to be locked already.

"Well maybe. I guess it's possible that Max would have gone up to inspect a stranger around the fish house, but she would have barked at a stranger. Maybe she would have gone in after someone, and that person got out and locked the door, but I don't know how anyone would have gotten in without the key. It's too much. Maybe Gordon did just lock her in."

Abby shook her head, as if trying to shake out the confusion that was forming cobwebs in her brain. "There are too many coincidences, Adam! I don't believe that the one night Gordon accidentally locks Max in the fish house, is the one night he goes off the wagon, drinks until he's staggering in spite of blood alcohol to the contrary, and falls into the lake where he drowns only a few feet from his dock. Someone had to have been here!"

"I don't know, Abby." Adam shook his head sadly. "I just don't know anymore, and I can't think about it right now. Fields of potatoes are waiting on me, so I'd better get going." Adam started walking toward the truck and opened the driver's door. Turning back he looked at her, a serious, deeply disturbed expression on his normally sunny face. "Abby, remember, if you're right, there's someone out there who will kill to get what he wants. If you're going to pursue this, you need to be careful. Make sure someone knows where you're going... speaking of which, what are you doing this afternoon?"

"No worries, Adam. I'll be careful. For now, I think I'm going to give Slimy Sommerfield a call."

Adam's mouth fell open as he stared at her with a shocked expression in his dark eyes. "What the... Why in the hell would you be giving Sommerfield a call?"

"Well, I thought I'd apologize for my rude behavior yesterday, and see if I can meet with him at his office to discuss things and to make amends. Maybe I was a bit hasty in the way I treated him yesterday," Abby said primly.

"I... You... I... Really Abby, are you thinking of selling the farm or developing it?" Abby didn't think that Adam's eyebrows could get any higher.

Abby made a moue of disgust. "No, actually I want a chance to look around his office and see if there's anything there that might tell me if he's the one who killed Uncle Gordon, or at least if he is involved."

"I thought we talked about this yesterday. There would be no point in him killing Gordon since he couldn't be sure he'd have a chance at the land."

"Yeah, well, he might have thought he'd have more chance to negotiate with an heir than he would with my uncle. Or, maybe he'd keep knocking people off until he got one willing to sell. He was acting pretty sketchy when he was talking about developing, and I want to see if I can find out why," Abby said stubbornly. "Besides, I have a tire that needs to be fixed. Jake said I shouldn't wait too long."

Adam took a deep breath, and shaking his head slowly he slid into the driver's seat of his truck. "Well, Abby, if you go over to Sommerfield's, take care. Better you than me. You might want to take a raincoat, since I'm guessing he's going to throw another load of pre-digested hay at you."

It took Abby a moment to process that comment in her head, then she grinned at Adam. Bullshit. "Don't worry, Adam. I'll take my muck boots!"

Waving, Adam drove down the driveway, heading for the potato fields.

Abby turned and walked into the house, holding the door for Max who was following closely. She wandered over to the kitchen table where she had left Sommerfield's business card the day before. Picking it up she went to the phone and dialed the numbers.

A woman's voice answered. "Reliance Real Estate. How can I help you?"

A few minutes later Abby had an appointment at 3:00 and directions to Sommerfield's Onaway office. She hung up the phone and glanced over at Max who was lying next to the table, chin on her crossed front paws, and eyes on Abby as usual.

"Hey Max, do you mind if I take the truck into Onaway this afternoon?" A sharp bark answered her question and Max jumped up and headed for the back door, claws clicking on the hardwood floor.

10

Shortly before three, Abby and Max pulled into a parking spot in front of an old, two-story red brick building that housed Sommerfield's real estate office. Rolling down the windows for the dog and mentally cursing her uncle's avoidance of such niceties as electric windows, Abby grabbed her purse, and mounted the concrete steps toward the large glass doors. A sign with the name *Reliance Real Estate* in electric blue and a particularly eye-searing shade of yellow hung in the window. Abby noticed that Sommerfield's name was the only one listed under the name. He must be the only broker in the office. Maybe that explained why he was pushing for a big deal like developing her lake.

Abby pushed the door open and stepped onto a large, airy room walled with pictures of various properties for sale. A large front bay window provided a wealth of natural light. Small spotlights over photos or artist's renderings of some of the more extravagant properties added their own illumination to the room. Abby paused for a moment and looked around the room, noting the empty chairs and end tables strewn with magazines and real estate brochures. Her eyes finally came to rest on the large desk along the back wall. No one was in sight.

"Hello?" Abby called, stepping farther into the room and closing the door behind her. A bell chimed, announcing her presence, she guessed.

A door opened on the far side of the room and a short,

pleasantly-rounded woman bustled through and paused, looking around. Spotting Abby, she smiled, and came forward, hand held out in a welcoming manner.

"Hello, you must be Ms. Williams. I'm Esther Cofield. We spoke on the phone?" Her tone invited Abby to remember the conversation, as though she would have forgotten having called only a couple of hours earlier.

"Hello Ms. Cofield." Abby smiled warmly, enjoying the older woman's warm, genuine personality. Whereas Sommerfield's greeting felt like icing on cardboard, Esther's was the real deal, a sweet greeting, covering a sweet personality. Abby had met enough fake people in her line of work to know genuineness when she saw it.

"Please, call me Esther." She beamed at Abby. "Mr. Sommerfield is on the phone with a client, but he should be off in just a moment. I'll just let him know that you're here."

"Thank you, Esther. I appreciate it."

Ms. Cofield bounced back to the dark wood paneled door, knocked once, and then opened it a crack, thrusting her head through.

"Mr. Sommerfield? Abby Williams is here for her three o'clock appointment."

An indecipherable mumble met Abby's ears, and Ms. Cofield pulled her head back out of the room and closed the door quietly.

"He says he'll just be a few more minutes. It's a very important client. Not that you're not, dear." Esther smiled at Abby. "Can I get you some coffee? Maybe some tea?" She gestured at a table under the bay window at the front of the building where two coffee urns and a stack of Styrofoam cups sat waiting alongside a plate of cookies. She looked so eager that Abby was afraid that refusing would hurt Esther's feelings. Considering the lack of sleep the previous night, Abby thought she just might be able to indulge in some late afternoon coffee without danger of insomnia.

"I'd love some coffee, Esther." Abby smiled back at the older woman who immediately headed for the table.

"Cream or sugar? We've got an absolutely wonderful coconut almond creamer here that I've become addicted to, truth to tell." Esther's smile took on a mischievous glint, and Abby found her own smile broadening in response.

"By all means, bring on the creamer. No sugar though, thank you." Abby accepted the steaming white cup from Esther and began to walk around the room, looking at the various properties as the older woman went back to her own desk.

Sommerfield certainly represented a large variety of properties, Abby thought, as she looked at images of large, modern lake front homes, and small farm houses. She came to a stop in front of a large artist's rendering of a development titled Loon Echo Estates. As she admired the artistry, she began to have an uncomfortable feeling that she'd seen this spot before.

The sound of a door opening pulled her attention away from the framed drawing and she turned to see Bill Sommerfield emerging from his office. He glanced around the room, and seeing Abby over near the rendering, he came forward warily.

Abby stepped forward hastily, not wanting Sommerfield to realize that she'd recognized the drawing as Lake Ellen, but a Lake Ellen that didn't exist, with houses and green lawns running down to the shore and docks jutting out into the water. She put out her hand to take Sommerfield's and shook it as she moved toward his office, causing him to turn away from the incriminating artwork.

"Hello, Mr. Sommerfield. I got thinking after you left, and I believe that I was hasty. Please forgive me. It's been so stressful with my uncle dying like that, and trying to handle his estate. I think I was unfair to you, and I wanted to apologize." Abby tried to project a "poor pitiful me" tone in her voice, gagging inwardly at how she sounded to herself.

Sommerfield visibly relaxed as he adopted a paternal air. "Don't worry at all, Ms. Williams. I understand perfectly. I imagine that it's been very overwhelming coming such a long distance. Believe me, all I want to do is help you in any way I can."

"To be honest, I guess I thought I should learn more about your proposition. I know my uncle really wanted me to stay on the farm, but I'm just not sure that's possible. As I'm sure you can imagine, I'm going to be hit with some pretty large estate taxes at the end of the year." Abby looked at Sommerfield with what she hoped was a helpless female aura.

It must have worked, as Sommerfield immediately smiled avuncularly, and took Abby's elbow to steer her toward his office door, and away from the drawing on the wall. "Yes, my dear. As I mentioned before, I have several investors who would be willing to give you a fair price for the property. You could even consider keeping the house itself as, say, a vacation home?" Sommerfield directed Abby to a large, overstuffed chair across from his desk, and then moved around to sit across from her.

"Thank you, Bill. I so appreciate your kindness in forgiving me for my earlier behavior."

Sommerfield shook his head gently, and ran the fingers of his right hand through his silvered hair in a self-conscious manner so pat that Abby was sure he practiced in front of the mirror, getting reading for his Man of the Year award.

"I believe that you said that you'd been working with my uncle for some time?"

"Yes, well, I'd been talking with Gordon about the possibility of developing part or all of his land. My investors are very eager, and would have paid your uncle well over farm value for the land."

"What was my uncle's view on the proposition?"

Sommerfield hesitated for a moment. "It was a good deal. I spoke to him a number of times about the situation."

"Then I take it he didn't sign a contract, or a binder, or you would be showing me that, correct?" Abby said, working hard to keep her voice neutral, instead of the hostile manner in which she'd brought up a signed contract the day before. She must have succeeded since Sommerfield's treacly smile remained unchanged.

"No, we were just at the beginning discussions. As I said, though, my investors are eager, and I'm sure that we would have come to an agreement soon. It was a very good deal for him."

"I see." Abby said. She was pretty sure that the translation of Sommerfield's statement was something like *Your uncle was holding out on us, but we would have worn him down*.

"So nothing had been done about the development yet? I mean no plans or anything?"

"No, no, no," Sommerfield blustered. "I have people interested, but we couldn't do anything yet since we didn't have access to a survey, topographical or geologic information in order to develop a plan."

"I noticed the artist's rendering of Loon Echo Estates out front. It looked a bit like Lake Ellen..." Abby paused, inviting Sommerfield to explain the drawing when he just told her that no work had been done planning the development.

"Oh that..." A look of panic lit Sommerfield's eyes. "These small lakes around here all look similar. I assure you that any similarity between it and your uncle's farm is purely coincidental. We...," a knock sounded at the door. Looking as though he'd just been reprieved, Sommerfield called out, "Yes Esther, what is it?"

The door opened and Esther's head popped around the

door. "Mr. Jameson is here. Apparently there's a problem with the inspection on the Nowicki house. He says he needs to speak with you right away."

A look of annoyance, mixed with a little of the "saved by the bell" type of relief, flashed across Sommerfield's face as he pushed back his chair. "I'll be right there Esther. If you'll excuse me for a moment Abby. I really need to check into this." Without waiting for a response, Sommerfield headed out of the room closing the door behind him.

Abby took a deep breath, and glanced over her shoulder toward the door. This was too good to be true. She scrambled to her feet and hurried around the desk. Looking at her options, she started by quickly thumbing through the papers stacked neatly on the side next to the large calendar.

Nothing there. It couldn't be that easy, could it? She glanced through the calendar, hoping to see something like "meeting with Gordon Dorsey." Still nothing. It appeared that other than a week long vacation in Colorado, Sommerfield hadn't had a lot of meetings on the books recently.

A scratching sound made her jump and she looked wildly around the room. The sound came again. A tree outside the window was waving in a light breeze, the branches scratching against the glass. Abby blew out a breath that she hadn't realized she was holding.

Crap, how do spies do this kind of work without having heart attacks on a daily basis?

Looking back at the door she tried to calculate how much time she might have before Sommerfield returned. Surely he wouldn't leave her alone in the office for very long.

From the desk she moved over to a series of standing files lined up on the table under the window itself. It was there that she hit pay dirt. Three folders in from the right hand side was one prominently labeled Loon Echo Estates. Sommerfield might have denied that the artist's rendering was of Lake Ellen, but she wasn't so sure.

Abby slid the file out and started looking through the paperwork inside. On the fourth page of the folder's contents she found a topographical map showing the details of roads and lot lines for the new subdivision. Cute woodsy names like Chipmunk Trail dotted the map, making Abby want to gag. Then one name jumped out at her. Lake Ellen.

That lying son of a bitch, Abby thought, gritting her teeth. *Loon Echo Estates is on Lake Ellen, and if he has this map, then he's been on the property surveying.* Abby wanted to take the folder and throw it in Sommerfield's conniving face, but instead grabbed her phone and snapped a picture of the map, and several other pages in the file, noting the name of the investment company developing Loon Echo Estates.

Well, if they thought they'd get ahold of her uncle's farm, she'd see about that. Abby slapped the folder shut and slid it back into the standing file, then picked up her purse and headed out the door.

Bill Sommerfield was on the far side of the main room shaking hands with a large, barrel-chested man with short-cropped sandy hair.

"Don't worry, Clyde, I'm sure that this inconsistency with the water report can be easily explained. I promise I'll get a hold of Mike right away so that we can get to the bottom of things. There's no need to pull the plug on the deal yet. You..." Sommerfield noticed that the man's attention had shifted to Abby when she opened the door. Sommerfield dropped the man's hand, and turned back to her.

"Ms. Williams... Abby! I apologize for leaving you waiting. I'm just finishing some business with Clyde Jameson here, and I'll be right back in."

"No worries, Bill. I appreciate your time, but I really have to be going. I've got Max out in the truck and it's getting toward chore time. Besides, I still need to get a tire fixed and I want to stop by Jenn Painter's shop." Abby gave Sommerfield a brilliant smile, praying he couldn't seen the churning anger in her guts. "Adam had a job over by... by... well some town starting with a 'P' and he wasn't sure if he would get back in time, so I may be on my own this evening." Abby knew she was babbling.

"Ah, I understand. I apologize again for not being able to spend more time with you. Hopefully we can talk again in the near future?" Sommerfield had regained the composure which had been shaken out of him earlier. Abby felt an irresistible urge to shake it again. Sort of how some people can't resist poking a bee hive with a stick... or throw stones at a bear.

As she was walking out the door, she suddenly stopped, and turning to Sommerfield, she said, "Just one thing, Bill. I was just sort of curious where you were when my uncle had his accident." Bullseye! Abby heard a squeak of in-drawn breath from Esther, and saw a frown of concentration crease Jameson's face. A look of total shock blasted Sommerfield's features.

"What the hell are you getting at, young lady?" Sommerfield sputtered. "The sheriff's department ruled Gordon's death an accident, or at least so I heard."

"That's what I'm told. I have just been wondering if he had some help with his 'accident.'" Abby tried to keep her voice in a light, non-committal range, and she saw a small twitch of a laugh cross the man, Jameson's, face.

"I don't know where you think you are, Ms. Williams, but this isn't the big city, and it sure isn't some 'Whodunit' that little miss Nancy Drew needs to solve."

Suddenly a shift came over Sommerfield and a sardonic half smile twisted his lips. "Besides, I wasn't even in town when your uncle died. I was out of town, attending a family reunion in Colorado, if you must know. You're going to have to look elsewhere for your 'help.'"

The balloon bubble high that Abby had been feeling over the success of her attack on Sommerfield suddenly deflated into a puddle on the ground as she remembered that page on his desk calendar. The one where the week was crossed out and the word "Colorado" written in bright red pen.

Damn, she should have caught that.

From the smug look on Sommerfield's face, he knew he'd scored a direct hit. Trying to muster whatever dignity she had remaining, she smiled at Sommerfield.

"I'm certainly glad to hear it, Bill. I'm sure you understand my wanting to learn everything I can about my uncle, and if we are to do business in the future..." The smug look shifted a little, as though he was worried that in his one-up-man-ship, he might have damaged his chances of getting the land. Abby felt a small thrill of redemption. Not enough to reinflate that balloon of self-confidence, mind you, but at least a little air was returning.

Abby opened the front door and hurried through, with Mrs. Cofield's "It was nice to meet you, dear" floating out after her.

12

Abby walked slowly back to the Dakota, her mind mulling over everything she'd just learned. Bill Sommerfield was obviously involved in something shady as far as the development was concerned. If he was to be believed, there was a lot of money involved. He certainly could have had a motive to murder her uncle if he thought he had a better chance of making a deal with the heirs. But he wasn't even in the state when Gordon died. Were there partners? Maybe one of whom would consider Gordon a barrier to making money? A lot of money?

Damn, damn, Abby thought. *Someone has to know something. I just have to keep looking,*

Abby was so deep in thought that when Max's head popped up in the window just as she put her hand on the door handle, Abby let out a scream and jumped backward, tripping and nearly falling on her butt. Feeling embarrassed, she glanced around to see if anyone was looking, and was immensely grateful to see the sidewalks empty.

"Max! You've got to stop doing that," Abby grumbled as she opened the truck door. Max jumped over to the passenger side of the truck and sat looking out the windshield. Abby slid in behind the wheel, backed out of the parking spot, and headed to the far side of town where Adam had told her she would find Onaway Tire City. She planned to drop off the truck and flat tire, then walk to

Jenn's shop which Adam said was only a block away on the other side of the street.

It only took a minute or two to make it from one end of town to the other, and not much longer to check in with the technicians of the tire store. Since she had Max with her, Abby told them just to fix the flat tire which was in the bed of the truck, but not to bother switching it with the spare. She figured that Adam could help her switch the tires around before they headed into town the next day.

The afternoon was rapidly cooling, and Tire City's parking lot was surrounded with trees which provided plenty of shade, so Abby felt comfortable rolling the windows partially up in order to spare the technician's nerves.

"Stay here, Max. I'll be right back."

Max looked at Abby and sneezed.

I'm so losing it, Abby thought, as she headed off down the street, looking for the old brick and clapboard single story building Adam described to her. Even knowing what she was looking for, she nearly missed the small consignment shop on the left hand side of the road. At the last moment she caught sight of the inset green-painted front door of Think Twice Consignment and Art. Looking both ways, and seeing nothing, she hurried across the street and headed for the entrance.

A small set of wind chimes tinkled as Abby pushed open the front door. The interior of the shop was cool, and the old building, with its low ceilings and plastered walls, had a pleasant, cozy cottage feeling. Abby paused inside the door and looked around. A variety of items were hung on racks or scattered on bookshelves throughout the room. It appeared that Jenn was a little more than a simple second hand shop, as many of the items appeared to be antiques, although Abby was far from versed in that area.

"Hello?" A voice sounded from a doorway at the back of the room.

"Hi, Jenn. Is that you? It's Abby."

"Hey Abby," came the disembodied voice. "My hands are tied up at the moment, come on back."

Abby wove her way through the racks and bookshelves toward the back of the room, noting as she went the beautiful items Jenn had displayed. She certainly had good taste, Abby thought, as she paused to examine a beautiful windblown wire sculpture of a tree, done in silver on an amethyst crystal base. A small metal plaque attached to the crystal identified the artist as Jenn herself.

"Wow. Hey Jenn, I didn't know you were an artist. I..." Abby's words stuttered to a stop as she stepped through the door into the back room. Looking around she saw a well-appointed artist's studio. The back wall was filled with large windows which let in plenty of natural light, while looking out into a small garden filled with wild flowers.

Jenn was seated at a tall table, holding a large wire sculpture onto a spiky chocolate brown crystalline rock. Looking more closely, Abby noted that the shape was of a mother and child, the two entwined, yet perfectly identifiable in spite of the medium.

"I'll be with you in just a moment, Abby," Jenn smiled at her. "I'm waiting for the epoxy to take.

"Don't worry about me. That's really amazing, Jenn. I had no idea that you were an artist. Your shop is beautiful too. I'm so envious. Any time I've tried some type of sculpture, it wound up looking a lot like those cow pies out in the pasture." Abby grinned at Jenn.

"That's me and clay. Adam says I'm not allowed to work on clay projects at home because it winds up everywhere, including dinner."

"Hey speaking of dinner, Adam invited me over Sunday evening. He said his mother was coming over and wanted to meet me."

A cloud obscured Jenn's naturally peaceful countenance. "Yeah, Gracie comes over once every week or two. She's lonely since Adam's father died, I think. She also spent a lot of time working with Adam when he was injured and lost his leg."

"Adam said she was a little possessive."

Jenn gave a sad little smile, eyes downcast. "She means well. Adam is her only child, and I'm sure it was terrifying when he was injured, especially so soon after Adam's dad was killed."

"Killed? What happened? I guess I assumed it was a heart attack or car wreck... something like that."

"It was a hunting accident, from what I understand. Adam doesn't like to talk about it much."

"What has she got against you? I'd think that she'd be thrilled that Adam's found someone."

"It's pretty complicated, but what it amounts to is she's pretty desperate for grandchildren, and I can't get pregnant."

"Oh." Abby wasn't sure what to say. She'd never had that burning desire for a baby that some of her friends described, but she'd also always assumed that some day she would have a family. She wasn't sure how she'd feel if she found out she could never have a child of her own.

"I'm so sorry," Abby said self-consciously.

"No, it's fine, Abby. It is what it is. Adam and I discussed the situation before we moved in together. It doesn't mean there aren't children in our future, they just won't be biologically ours."

Abby wasn't sure how to respond, so she didn't say anything for several moments.

"So, what brings you into town this afternoon?" Jenn asked, apparently deciding that it was high time for a change of subject.

"I just got done visiting Bill Sommerfield over at Reliance Realty."

"Really?" Jenn looked at Abby as though she'd grown a second head and both were having a bad hair day.

"Really." Abby chuckled at the look on Jenn's face.

"I thought Adam said that you had a bit of a run in with Sommerfield yesterday."

"I did. But then I got thinking that Sommerfield had the perfect motive for killing my uncle if he wanted to develop the farm the way he said. I decided that I needed to check him out a little more thoroughly, so I called and told him I was considering selling the farm."

"Are you? Considering selling the farm, I mean."

Abby paused for a moment, an uncomfortable feeling in the pit of her stomach. "I don't know, Jenn. I think right now I'm just focused on finding out how my uncle wound up in the water. I know it's not as simple, open-and-shut as the sheriff's department would like me to believe."

"Did you learn anything new?"

"Have you ever heard of Loon Echo Estates?"

Jenn looked confused. "No, is it near here? What does it have to do with Gordon?"

Abby pulled out her phone and called up the picture of the map she'd found in the folder in Sommerfield's office. Spreading her fingers to enlarge the picture to the point that the name of the lake was easily readable, Abby then handed the phone over to Jenn.

"That's Loon Echo Estates."

"But that's Lake Ellen. There's no development there. Your uncle would never allow it. There must be some sort of mistake."

"I think the only mistake is that Sommerfield jumped the gun, and somehow got a survey of the land and started the planning stages of the development. Honestly, there's a huge artist's rendering in the front room of his office."

"So he killed your uncle why? Because he thought he might be able to get the land from you?"

"That's what I thought, but the problem is that he was

in Colorado during that week, at least according to his desk calendar... and him." Abby's face twisted in remembrance of his scorn when informing her of his whereabouts at the time of Gordon's death.

"Maybe one of his partners?"

"Possibly. I just don't really know. He said he had investors interested in the land, but I've got a sneaky suspicion that he may be exaggerating that as well."

"You need to be careful, Abby. If you're right, and someone killed your uncle, that someone might not appreciate your looking into the accident. I bought my shop from Sommerfield about three years ago, and he gave me the creeps."

"Don't worry, Jenn. I'll be careful. But I'm not going to stop either." Abby set her jaw, determined more than ever to find out what happened when her uncle died.

13

Chores were done a bit late that evening. The animals were not amused, as their raised voices attested to when Abby drove into the barnyard at 6:30. Everyone was at the fence nickering, mooing, bleating or otherwise making a ruckus. She didn't hear anything from the trout, but she figured that even they were uttering fishy curses.

Even though she'd only intended to stop by Jenn's shop for a few minutes just to say hi while the tire was being fixed, she wound up staying until Jenn closed at 5:00, and even then the two stood talking for another fifteen minutes or so.

Finally, Jenn pointed out how silly it was that they were standing on the sidewalk taking when they were living fewer than two minutes from each other, besides the animals would be waiting. Glancing at her watch, Abby realized she only had a few minutes to make it back to Tire City before it closed, and giving Jenn a quick wave took off down the street. She made it back to the store with five minutes to spare and paid for the fix.

She and Max headed out, making one quick stop at the grocery store to pick up a couple of items which Abby had forgotten on her trip in to Rogers City the day before. Aware that she was going to be late, and not sure if Adam had made it back for chores, Abby pushed the accelerator down under the decidedly critical stare of Max. At least Abby felt that the dog's look was disapproving of her tardiness.

As Abby steered the truck down the two-rut gravel drive past Adam and Jenn's house, she mentally crossed her fingers that Adam had made it back and started chores. She still wasn't confident that she would remember everything, and since she was late anyway... well, it would be nice to have the company.

No red truck sat in front of the barn, however, when Abby came through the narrow band of forest between the county road and the farm. She was on her own.

"Okay, Max. Let me go put on my chore clothes, and we'll get going."

Max had no comment, but then Abby figured she was so disgusted with the situation that she was giving Abby the silent treatment.

Abby practically jumped into the dirty jeans and t-shirt she'd worn that morning while cleaning the fish. She needed to do a load of laundry. She shook her head. Damn, she'd only been here three days now, and already she'd gone through most of her wardrobe... or at least the wardrobe suitable for farm life. If she was going to stay longer, she'd need to pick up some more clothes... or figure out how to stay cleaner.

The goats, cattle and horses were cared for, their water tanks filled, the chickens checked, and the fish fed when Adam finally drove into the barnyard.

"It's about time you showed up, you shirker." Abby grinned at Adam as he climbed out of the truck covered in mud and grease.

"Oh, yeah, I've been doing nothing all afternoon. So how did the chores go?"

"You're just in time to milk the goat. That's the only thing left. I got a late start because I went in to Onaway to see Sommerfield, and then stopped to see Jenn's shop while I was waiting for the flat tire to be fixed. I wound up spending more time there than I thought."

"Great. It sounds like you've got it under control. I

wouldn't want to deprive you of the success of your first chore session on your own." Adam laughed at Abby's rueful expression.

"I take it you're not milking the goat?"

"Nah, you've got it."

"You can't blame a girl for trying can you?" Abby headed back into the barn, closely followed by Max, who'd been shadowing her throughout all the farm duties. Abby had caught herself taking to the dog as she did the chores, which she guessed wasn't that unusual, until of course she realized she'd been telling Max about her problems with Josh, and her dilemma about staying on the farm or returning to Phoenix. It dawned on Abby that she was slightly disappointed when the pooch had no suggestions. It was then that she realized that she'd totally lost her mind.

"How did your visit with Sommerfield go?" Adam asked, catching up with her at the open door of the barn.

"It was interesting. Do you know anything about a development called Loon Echo Estates?"

"No. Sounds like one of those places where the down staters come to for their vacations. Sounds like just the thing that Sommerfield would have in mind for this place."

"Jenn hadn't heard of it either."

"So where is it?"

"From what I understand, it's all around you." Abby gestured with her arm, indicating all the land around with a big sweeping motion. "I saw the plat at Sommerfield's, along with a very nice artist's rendering of the development."

"You must be mistaken. There's no way Gordon would have agreed to anything like that, and they would have had to have his permission in order to survey and develop the plan." Adam's eyes narrowed. "Wait a minute. Are you saying that Sommerfield, or someone connected to

Sommerfield snuck in here without permission, surveyed and developed the plan? That would be foolish beyond sanity. A lot of money would be wrapped up into something like that, and if Gordon couldn't be persuaded to sell, all that money would go right down the toilet."

"That's what I thought. The problem is, however, that Sommerfield was out of town when Uncle Gordon drowned, and I bet he has the t-shirt to prove it, or he wouldn't have looked so smug when he told me about his alibi. I thought maybe a partner..."

"Have you told the sheriff's department yet? Maybe called that Deputy Morrison you spoke with?"

"There hasn't been time." Abby felt her jaw tighten. "Besides, he didn't seem too concerned when I talked to him earlier."

"But now you have real information. You have proof there was something going on that could have put Gordon in the cross hairs. You need to fill him in, and let the department take over the investigation." Adam reached out and took Abby's upper arm, turning her to face him.

"Maybe I'll give him a call tomorrow." Abby said, catching a petulant tone in her voice, and ashamed of it. She knew he was right, but she was just as sure that the sheriff's department wouldn't take her seriously if she told them what she found out. She didn't meet Adam's eyes.

Adam shook his head, and turned into the barn.

"I'll go get Autumn while you get the milking equipment ready."

The remainder of the chores were done in a stiff silence that didn't loosen until after the milk was cared for and the two were headed back out across the barnyard toward Adam's truck.

Angry at herself and afraid she'd damaged her new friendship in its formation, she finally took several quick steps and blocked Adam's forward motion.

"Adam stop." Abby looked up at him. "I will call Deputy Morrison. I promise. You're right. If someone killed Gordon to get his land, I could be next. I get that."

Adam took a deep breath and his features softened.

"Abby, your uncle was like a father to me, and a best friend. He's the only person I've ever known who I really felt understood what it was like when I came home, injured and depressed. He knew the nightmares, and the flashbacks, and the pain. He understood the struggle involved in taking back my life. It hurt like hell when he died, and it hurt even worse because of the way he died. You were important to him, and if something happens to you, I'll feel like I let him down.

"I don't know if someone killed your uncle. It would almost make it easier if it happened that way. But if it did, then I don't want to see the same thing happen to you."

Abby watched Adam's face carefully, seeing the rawness and pain left there by not only her uncle's death, but by all the other things that had happened in his life, and all the other people he'd lost.

"Don't worry, Adam. I'll call Deputy Morrison, and I'll stay away from Sommerfield. But Adam, if my uncle was killed over the land and I also refuse to sell the farm for development, I might be next."

"All the more reason to let Morrison know what you've found out." Adam gave Abby a crooked smile.

"Now, on to more enjoyable topics. I'll pick you up tomorrow morning at seven-thirty, and we'll head into Alpena for the farmer's market."

"You call seven thirty 'enjoyable' do you?" Abby looked at him squint eyed. "I take it that all the chores have to be done before we leave."

"Can't very well do them after we leave can you?" All the worry was gone from Adam's face and he grinned at Abby's expression of distaste.

"Fine. I'll get up at the crack of dawn to feed the hoards

so that I can then pack fish into town. Good grief, what has my life become?"

"It's a good life, Abby. You'll find out if you stay." Adam got into his truck and headed for home.

"Come on Max," Abby said to her canine shadow. "Time to get us fed. Where's that dang cat?" Abby looked around and then called "kitty, kitty, kitty" and was rewarded to see Cali Cat come racing out of the barn, pause briefly looking around, then run over to them.

"Good, we're all here now. Move 'em out."

As Abby and her entourage proceeded to the back door, she contemplated her promise to Adam. She'd call Morrison. Maybe she should call tonight and leave a message.

She stood just inside the kitchen looking at the phone, chewing her lip. Maybe she'd also call Rick Laskis. As a lawyer, maybe he'd know how to find out who was working with Sommerfield on Loon Echo Estates. Researching from a distance wouldn't be the same as going near Sommerfield, so she'd be keeping her promise to Adam.

Abby searched through the drawer next to the phone, looking for Rick's business card. Glancing at the embossed silver and green finish, she picked up the receiver and started punching in numbers.

14

This time an alarm was the herald of morning, and not a dog and cat combo. The night before Abby set the alarm on her cell phone for the ungodly hour of 5:00 a.m. She'd searched high and low, but apparently Gordon hadn't believed in alarm clocks along with his disavowal of computers and the Internet.

Abby opened her eyes to the incessant chiming of the phone, reached out and hit the dismiss icon, and turned on the bedside lamp. At the same time she heard a wild scrabbling of claws on the far side of the room where Max seemed to like to sleep in front of the open window. There was a thump on the end of the bed, and Abby looked over to see Cali Cat sitting there nonchalantly, as though she'd been there the whole time. Max appeared around the corner of the bed, looking slightly wild-eyed in Abby's opinion.

A smug feeling of satisfaction came over Abby. She'd won one! For once Max, the super dog, had been taken off guard and Abby woke her in the morning instead of the other way around.

"How do you like it when the fur is on the other foot, Max?"

Max looked at her with a slightly resentful expression. At least Abby thought it was resentful. On the other hand, Abby thought, it probably said something about Abby herself, that she felt herself in competition with a dog. Abby's feeling of victory started to fade, replaced with a vague guilty feeling that she'd scared Max.

"Okay, I'm sorry Max. It was just the alarm. See?" Abby pushed several icons on the phone's surface causing it to play the alarm tone. Max's ears perked up, and her head tipped to the right, then the left, as if trying to determine exactly what that thing was that was making such strange sounds. Abby held the phone out toward Max, and after a moment of intense scrutiny, she sniffed it then returned to studying Abby.

"Okay, girl? I'm sorry if I scared you, but it's all good." Abby reached out, but once again, Max ducked her head, avoiding the fingers. The feeling of guilt faded. "Fine. Just fine, Max. You know sooner or later you've got to accept it's just me now. Gordon's gone." Abby's throat started to tighten and her eyes stung in an unexpected surge of emotion. "Gordon's gone and you're stuck with me, and we're going to have to learn how to get along!"

Max continued to study Abby with no reply. Feeling defeated, Abby sighed and stood up, heading for the bathroom. Adam was going to be there at 7:30, and she wanted to get the chores done, be showered and ready by the time he got there.

Two and a half hours later Adam, Abby and Max, as well as 120 trout, were loaded in the Dakota and heading for the farmer's market in Alpena. The plan was to hit The Beaches first, drop off their order, and then proceed to the vacant lot where the market was held Friday through Sunday every week of the summer.

Adam's deep freeze from the evening before seemed to have thawed, and Adam and Abby talked companionably for the majority of the drive. Adam was a wealth of funny stories about Gordon and his life on the farm, and by the end of the trip Abby felt like she knew her uncle in a way she never had before, considering the shallowness of their connection over the years.

The two were still laughing as they drove into the empty parking lot in front of a flagstone and white plaster restaurant facing Thunder Bay. Adam drove around the right side of the building to the kitchen entrance. The door opened and a huge man wearing a black t-shirt and jeans stepped out. Adam hit the parking brake and opened the driver's door, stepping out into the cool morning air scented by the lake breezes.

"Adam! How's it going?" The large man called out. He came forward; hand thrust out and grabbed Adam's, pumping it vigorously. "Is this the new owner? Gordon's niece?" The man gestured toward Abby who'd gotten out of the truck on the passenger side and started walking around the hood of the truck toward the pair of men.

"Hi, Abby. I'm pleased to meet you. I'm Raymond Davidson. Ray."

"Hello, Ray, it's great to meet you."

"The pleasure is all mine. I was so sorry to hear about your uncle. Gordon was a great guy, and he sure knew how to raise a fish." Ray gave her a huge grin as he pumped her hand up and down. "Are you planning on staying and keeping the fish farm running?"

"I haven't decided what I'm going to do yet, Ray. I've only been here a few days, and there's a lot to learn."

"Adam can teach you. Besides, from a purely selfish standpoint, I want to keep getting your trout for my restaurant. You guys raise the best product around. My basil cilantro baked trout with lemon just isn't the same with any other fish." Ray's enthusiasm was infectious, and Abby found herself grinning in return. "Mind you it's great regardless, but with your fish... mmmmuum. The best. Gordon always said it was the water. That his well produced water with just the right temperature and mix of minerals."

"Hey Ray, let's get your fish unloaded. We need to head over to the farmer's market and get set up. Besides,

I need to get you to stop scaring off Abby. We want her to stay, not run screaming from the state." Adam gestured toward the back of the truck where the coolers were riding.

"Alright, alright. I'm not scaring Abby away, am I Abby? It would take more than little 'ole me to scare her." Ray chuckled deep in his chest and his grin was undiminished as he turned back into the kitchen, and emerged almost immediately with a large bin for the fish he selected. He examined Abby with a direct gaze that made Abby feel both refreshed and exposed at the same time.

"No. You haven't scared me away. But everything here is so strange after living in Phoenix for so many years. I'm sure not used to having to plan my whole day around needing to go grocery shopping. Back in Phoenix, I'd just stop at any of a number of stores on the way home from work. Here I have to plan a major expedition."

"Don't worry, you'll get used to it." Ray patted her on the shoulder, his huge hands feeling like a hammer determined to pound her into the ground. "I moved here from New York, where I grew up. It was culture shock to be sure, but it was worth it!"

Ray turned away and started sorting through the fish in the coolers, examining each one before he either placed it in his bin, or put it back into the cooler. Abby got the distinct impression that he was interviewing each one to determine whether it was worthy of his refined taste. She felt a giggle start to bubble up inside her, and stomped it down firmly. She wasn't sure if Ray would be offended, but she was sure that she didn't want to lose The Beaches' business.

It didn't take long for Ray to find the sixty-five trout he wanted for that evening's special and Abby and Adam were able to drive the few miles to the large empty parking lot that housed the farmer's market. Already half a dozen shades had been erected and tables set up. People were busy setting out various types of vegetables and fruits grown in the area. One table was filled with a display of apples which made Abby's mouth water. Another table was covered with a table cloth covered with goofy-looking cartoon chickens. A large ceramic hen stood in the middle of the table, with a sign propped up against here advertising farm fresh chicken and duck eggs.

Adam pulled into a spot at the end of the line of tents, backed in so that the rear of the truck faced the same direction as all the other vendor's tables, and turned off the truck.

"Grab the cash box will you Abby? Come on Max." Adam got out of the truck, holding the door for the dog to follow. On the passenger side, Abby reached in the back for the cash box, then got out herself and walked to the back where Adam was already pulling Gordon's folded popup shade out of the bed of the truck.

"What do you want me to do, Adam? How can I help?"

"Set the cashbox down, and help me with the tent."

Abby set the cashbox in the bed of the truck, figuring that Max would keep an eye on it, and helped Adam finish sliding the popup out of the bed. The two of them stretched out the legs until the canopy was stretched out tight. Grabbing the back legs of the popup, the two of them slid the tent back over the bed of the truck, providing shade for the coolers, as well as Max who was laying on a folded tarp near the cab. Adam then reached into the bed and pulled out two folding chairs and a table, which he set up behind the tailgate, close to the front of the shade. Finally he grabbed a heavy plastic tote and pulled out a scale, and several rolls of heavy plastic wrap and butcher paper.

"We're all set, I guess." Adam looked over the setup, then at Abby. "Now the real fun begins." Adam turned around and sat in the chair on the left hand side of the tailgate, and crossed his feet.

Abby gave him a skeptical look from the corner of her eye. "That's how you do it around here?"

"Yep. At this point it's pretty much sit here until someone shows up wanting to buy some fish. It might be a bit slow today as no one has been here since before Gordon's accident and Fridays are always slower than Saturdays, but we should be able to clear out the number of fish we brought."

"I take it Gordon never had any kind of reservation process?"

"No, it was always first come first serve, although there were times someone would ask a week before, or give him a call and ask for a certain number or weight of fish. That was the exception instead of the rule, however."

"What about the other trout farm you mentioned?"

"They don't usually come to the farmer's market. They do run a 'You catch 'em, we clean 'em' program there. I'm told it's pretty popular. Most of the time they'll only come in for the farmer's market when they have a bunch of fish already at processing size, and the next batch ready to move into the adult pond. Trout are pretty picky about water quality, and you don't want to overcrowd them."

Abby chewed her lip, thinking about what passed as her uncle's business model. "You know, I could build a website, and take orders through it, maybe even make special deliveries like you do for the restaurants. It would help us be more accurate in processing the correct number of fish for the farmer's market as well. We could even send out a weekly newsletter with recipes and cooking suggestions to people on an email mailing list. That way if we had a larger number of fish that needed processing, we could send out specials. We..." Abby looked up to see Adam watching her, a smile lurking around his lips.

"Sounds like you're planning on staying awhile?"

"I...," Abby juttered to a stop, confused. "I guess maybe I am." *Damn, I've been here less than a week and I'm already thinking about totally upending my whole life?*

Abby collapsed into the other folding chair, feeling shell shocked. She sat there, staring off into the distance, her head swimming. Fear and excitement both vied for control. So many thoughts were swirling around in her head that it took a moment for a new voice to penetrate the fog and return her to reality.

"Adam. Hi. We've missed you guys the last few weeks." A small blonde woman approached the table, a big welcoming smile on her face.

"Hey Penny. It's good to see you." Adam reached out and took the woman's hand. "Abby, this is Penny Jackson. She's one of the best bakers around and usually has a booth here, down at the end."

"Adam's buttering me up." Penny grinned at Abby. "I make a sourdough bread that he's addicted to, and yes, Adam, I have some today. I'll put a loaf away for you, shall I?" Penny kept stealing glances at Abby out of the corner of her eye while she was talking with Adam.

"You bet. Two if you have them. Penny, this is Abigail Williams, Gordon's niece. Looks like she's going to be taking over the farm."

"At least for the time-being," Abby inserted hastily, still not ready to commit whole-heartedly to the idea.

"Oh my gosh, Adam. Abby. I was so sorry to hear about Gordon's accident." Penny shook her head in sorrow. "Your uncle was such a good man. I used to bake several extra loaves of cinnamon raisin swirl just for him."

"I'll have to get some and see what had him hooked, if you have any with you today." Abby smiled at Penny, liking the woman's bouncy, cheerful attitude. She reminded Abby of Lucy even though the two couldn't have looked more different from each other. Abby herself tended to be a bit more reserved and goal driven and she'd missed Lucy's ability to help her balance her life the last few days.

"I most certainly have some. I'll put a loaf back with

Adam's sourdough and you can pick it up later. While I'm here, though, I'd like to get four fish for tonight's dinner. Can you put them aside in the cooler? I didn't know you were going to be here, so I didn't bring a cooler myself."

"Certainly. "Adam beckoned her around the table to where the large coolers sat in the bed of the truck. "Why don't you pick out the four you want, and we'll wrap them in a plastic bag and set them to the side."

"Fantastic. Tom, my husband," Penny clarified for Abby, "Tom loves it when I bring fresh trout home for dinner after farmer's market. He says it saves him the time of going out and catching them himself. Like he thinks it's a chore!" Penny laughed heartily and Abby couldn't help grinning in response.

After Penny's visit to the table, the rest of the morning was fairly busy. A number of other vendors stopped by whenever there was down time so that they could offer their condolences to Adam and Abby. Most knew Gordon well as he was the one who was usually at the market, but Adam was also very familiar to the crowd.

Many customers also stopped by, professing how happy they were to see the fish back at the market, and the level of trout in the coolers steadily dropped as the morning progressed.

She had just finished packing two beautiful speckled trout for an older woman pulling a wagon loaded with her purchases when Abby looked up to see Rick waiting patiently at the table.

"Hey Adam? Do you mind if I take a quick break? I need to go over a couple of things with Rick."

Adam, who was talking with Clive, the young bearded man from the wood working booth three spaces down from theirs, nodded in her direction and moved back closer to the table without pausing in his conversation.

"Just a second, Rick. Let me grab my purse."

Abby walked quickly to the front of the truck and reached under the front seat for her tablet case and tucked it into the drawstring backpack she'd chosen to use as a purse since it would hold the tablet without being obvious. She slung the straps over her shoulder and hurried back to where Rick was standing, talking with Adam and Clive.

"We won't be gone long, Adam. Are you sure it's okay?"

"No worries, Abby. I've got it." Adam waved Rick and Abby away and turned to greet several customers who were just approaching the table.

"Come on Rick." Abby pulled Rick with her, and headed down to the end of the rows of shades.

"Abby, slow down," Rick called, hurrying to catch up with her. "Where are we going?"

"There's a little coffee shop on the far side of the parking lot. I thought we could go there."

"That will work, but what's all this about. When you called last night you said that you thought Gordon had been killed, and that you might know why. I..."

"Shhh. We're still too close. I don't want anyone in the farmer's market to hear what I have to say and ask Adam about it."

Rick came to a stop in the middle of the parking lot. "Abby, what the hell is going on? Your uncle had an accident. He drowned. It was a tragedy, but it was an accident, not a murder conspiracy."

Abby turned, looking over Rick's shoulder to see if anyone in the line of popups and tables was paying any attention to them. Fortunately there seemed to be a wave of customers descending on the market, and she couldn't see anyone looking in their direction.

"Rick, I'll explain everything in a moment, but believe

me, I did find something that could be a motive for someone to kill my uncle. I need your help, though."

Rick gave Abby a skeptical look, but finally started moving in her direction again, and together they finished the short distance to the coffee shop.

A bell chimed as Rick pushed the door to the Coffee Cup coffee shop open and held it for Abby to enter. The smell of coffee and baked goods met her nose like a cloud.

"Do you want something?" Rick asked.

"Uh, yeah." Abby studied the menu board mounted on the wall behind the service counter. "Can I get a cinnamon latte?"

"Sure. Why don't you find us a table?" He swept his arm indicating the nearly empty coffee shop. "And I'll get our drinks."

Abby wandered over to a table situated next to the window near the back of the room, pulled out a chair and sat down. She pulled the tablet out of the backpack and pushed the power button, waiting for it to wake up to the sign in window. She glanced over to where Rick was standing at the counter talking with the young girl operating the cash register. She looked down to see the log on window and entered her password.

"Here you go." Abby looked up to see Rick standing there with two cups of coffee. She moved her tablet aside and he set one marked CIN in black marker in front of her.

"Thanks, Rick." Abby pulled the cup close, and took a deep breath of the fragrant steam curling up from the brim and closed her eyes. *Ahhh. Do I really want to move to a farm, and miss this every day?*

She opened her eyes to see Rick watching her with a wry smile twisting his features. He took a sip from his cup, and then set it down on the table in front of him.

"Okay, Abby, now what gives?"

"Did my uncle ever talk to you about being approached

by people who wanted to buy his farm to develop it into vacation homes?"

Rick looked surprised. "Well, yes, he mentioned several times that he'd been made offers. It seemed like every few months he'd either get a letter or a real estate agent or developer would stop by or phone wanting to make him an offer. He usually hung up on them, ordered them off the property, or tore up the letters. He wasn't interested. Why? Are you thinking of selling to one of these guys?"

"No. Actually I'm thinking of staying." Abby frowned and tugged on the light brown ponytail hanging over her shoulder. "The other day a real estate agent named Bill Sommerfield stopped by to introduce himself. He claimed that he'd been talking to Uncle Gordon about developing. I sort of ran him off myself, but then I got thinking that if there was as much money in the development as he was implying, there also might be a reason to remove any blockage to progress. A blockage like my uncle."

"Okay, I follow you so far."

"So I called and made nice, and set up an appointment to meet him at his office."

"I'd have liked to see that," Rick chuckled, his blue eyes sparkled with laughter.

"Yeah, well I wish you had. He had this huge artist's rendering in the office. It looked like Lake Ellen, but the legend at the bottom called it Loon Echo Estates."

Rick's attention had sharpened perceptibly.

"So, I was left in the office for a few minutes when someone came by who needed to talk to Sommerfield. I found a folder with some papers." Rick gave her a skeptical look at the word "found" but Abby ignored it and continued. "I photographed some of them. Here." Abby thrust the tablet out toward Rick, with the photo of the development map enlarged.

Rick studied the photo, using his finger to move the photo around and enlarge portions.

"If you scroll through, you'll see pictures of some of the other documents."

Rick looked up from the tablet. "Abby, you know you shouldn't have been looking through this folder."

"Yeah, well they shouldn't have been on Gordon's property and surveying Gordon's land, so I'm guessing the score is even at the moment. What do you think?"

"Other than you were potentially trespassing, maybe breaking a couple of laws, as well as aggravating a potential murderer? I think that there's something pretty shady going on, and although I really hate to admit it, I think you may have discovered a potential motivation for your uncle to be killed. Of course, they may have used a drone in order to get a closer look at the property and based the rendering and the development plan on that preliminary to a full survey, but even that is pretty expensive. The upside, however, is that it would be difficult to get charged for a trespass. Have you contacted the sheriff's department? I'm guessing one of the reasons they put it down to accidental death was that no one knew of anybody who might have a grudge against your uncle."

"Yeah, I called them last night." Abby dismissed the question. She most certainly did call the night before, right after she called Rick, and left a message on Morrison's voice mail. The fact that she hadn't talked to him directly, and didn't intend to follow up on the call until she had more information was beside the point in her book.

"The problem is that Sommerfield was in Colorado, so he couldn't have done it, and I guess I don't buy the whole 'hired hit man' scenario. I was hoping you could help me find Sommerfield's partners or investors, or whoever might also have a stake in this development."

Rick studied the pictures again, zooming in on the lower left-hand corner of the platt. "Look here." He indicated a small line of writing that Abby had missed when she'd examined the map earlier. "It says LEE Development,

LLC. That means that the creators of the map, this LEE Development, are a 'limited liability company.' That means that they must have registered, and that the information for the registration of the LLC is public record."

"So I can just go online, look up the company and it will tell me all the owners?"

"Yes..." Rick sounded wary as he examined Abby's face carefully, his dark brown eyes serious. "But Deputy Morrison will be investigating all of this information. Do you want to tell me exactly what's going on?"

"Morrison could have looked for my uncle's killer weeks ago, but instead everyone just said it was an accident." Abby took a sip of her coffee and fought to get her temper under control. "I don't know, I just have a feeling that if they try and sweep it under the rug again, I want to know more details other than 'we've talked with those involved and there's no evidence of foul play.'"

"Abby, I agree that there might be a motive for murder here, but it could also just be some greedy people hoping to cash in on a development deal, and Gordon's accident is just an unhappy coincidence. You've uncovered some unethical dealings here, to be sure, but nothing more at this time, and you're not an investigator. If you keep up, you could potentially damage any real evidence of wrong doing. You need to let the sheriff's department handle this." Rick's voice was serious and his eyes seemed to bore holes into her head."

"Don't worry, Rick. I'll let Morrison have the whole thing. I just want to know what's happening. If I poke around on the computer it won't make any difference."

Rick shook his head, took a final sip of his coffee, and stood. Handing the tablet back to Abby, he said, "Well, I've given you my two cents worth; make sure you keep my card with you for when you need someone to bail you out of jail. Now, if we're done, I'd like to go pick up a few trout before they're all taken."

Abby powered off the tablet and slipped it into her bag, grabbed the half empty cup of coffee, and joined Rick in heading out the door and back across the parking lot.

Business was brisk, and by 2:30 Adam and Abby were sold out of fish and Abby had started taking the names and phone numbers of people who'd gotten there too late to buy. Adam told her that Gordon had traditionally come to the market the last Friday of each month, unless he had extra fish and needed to clear out the adult pond in preparation for a new batch of maturing juveniles.

Abby was surprised how tired she was as she helped Adam pack the popup, table and other equipment back into the truck and found herself wishing that she could go home, put up her feet, and eat a pint of rocky road ice cream, not feed a farm full of animals.

They made a quick stop on the way out of town so that Abby could pick up a small computer printer and a mobile hotspot, and the two, with Max in tow, headed out Hwy. 32 on their way back out to the farm. The ride was quiet, and Abby found she kept nodding off. She was surprised when Adam turned off the county road onto the dirt road, since she couldn't remember having passed any of her landmarks.

A few minutes later Adam backed the Dakota up to the front of the barn and turned off the truck. As Abby opened the door, Max squeezed past and ran into the barn. Apparently out of nowhere, Cali Cat appeared and ran full speed into the barn after Max.

"I take it they're late for an important farm meeting," Abby said almost to herself.

Adam on the other side of the truck heard her and laughed. "No, Max just wants to make sure that nothing has happened to her farm while she was in town, and Cali Cat just wants to make sure that nothing happened to Max."

Adam and Abby unpacked the back of the pickup, and cleaned and disinfected the coolers then carried them back up to the fish house and stored them behind the door. Standing back in front of the barn the two were silent for a moment, each lost in his or her own thoughts.

Finally Adam turned and looked at Abby. "Are you good for chores this evening? You did a great job last night, and since you're going to stay..."

"*Maybe* going to stay," Abby said, still not willing to commit one hundred percent.

Adam laughed. "...*Maybe* going to stay, you might as well get accustomed to the job. I thought I might take Jenn out for dinner in Millersburg tonight, since she's going to have to put up with my mother on Sunday, and I have to work all day tomorrow. You're still coming for dinner, right?"

"Not having to cook...wouldn't miss it for the world." Abby yawned. "Yeah, I think I can handle the chores, and if I have a question, I can always call you."

With that, Adam got in his truck and headed back to the house on the road.

Abby stood a moment longer, stretching her back and neck, then headed for the house, determined to get a drink, and take it easy for a few minutes before starting on the chores. A clatter of gravel and flurry of activity startled her as Max and Cali Cat went tearing by at a dead run apparently aiming for the back door of the house. Max was carrying something in her mouth which looked way too much to Abby like a dead rat.

"Max! What the heck! Drop that!" Max spun, kicking up small stones, and ran back toward Abby, causing her to jump in panic.

"Knock it off Max!" Abby shrieked sure that the dog was going to push the dead thing onto her leg the way she had with the piece of flannel two days before. While Abby was prepared to deal with cows and horses, and even fish, she drew the line at dead rats being shoved at her.

Instead, however, Max dropped her prize at Abby's feet, and backed off, eyes never wavering from Abby, as if to see what she'd do now. Abby's nose wrinkled in disgust, as she looked down at the thing Max placed in her path. She couldn't leave it here, obviously. Who knew what Max would do with this prize next.

Peeking from narrowed eyes, as if not seeing the rat clearly would make it go away, she tried to determine the best way to remove the body from the path, without having to actually touch the thing. As she was pondering her actions, Cali Cat approached, reached out one white paw, and to Abby's dismay, flipped the dead animal over and toward her.

"Cat!" Abby jumped back, hazel eyes open wide as she looked at the "rat" at her feet. What she'd thought was a dried up flattened carcass turned out to be a dirty glove which had apparently seen better days. It was stained dark, stiff and wrinkled, having apparently been exposed to water. Cali Cat batted at it again, sliding the glove across the ground a few more inches, then suddenly lost interest and started to wash her face.

Abby's heart rate began to return to normal, and she reached out a toe to turn the glove over again, then, still hesitating as though it was going to come alive, she reached down to pick up the piece of leather with two fingers.

A soft woof from Max made her look in that direction. The dog was sitting, watching her every move with those unnerving eyes.

"Okay, Max, so what do you want me to do with this?" Remembering what happened when she threw the piece of material the other day, she hung onto the glove with two fingers. She supposed it could be one of the dog's toys... an old glove for which the mate had disappeared.

But, if so, why didn't she want Abby to throw it for her. Maybe Max was finally beginning to accept Abby's existence and was bringing her a gift... a nasty, dirty, smelly gift.

"Okay, dog. If this is a peace offering, I accept." Abby shook the glove, causing small bits of dirt to fly all over. "But next time see if you can find me diamond earrings okay?" She stood for a moment, trying to decide what to do with the glove, finally sighed and took it into the house with her. The scrap of green flannel was still sitting on the counter next to the door, and Abby placed the glove on top of the rag. It appeared small for one of her uncle's gloves, but maybe it was Jenn's. She'd have to ask her the next time they met.

"I'm going to have a heck of a collection soon, Max. It's not that I don't appreciate the thought, but I'm thinking we're good now."

Abby turned to look at Max, only to realize that she'd already left the room, heading down the basement stairs to her food and water bowls, Cali Cat hot on her heels. Abby rolled her eyes and blew out a breath. She was never going to get used to that dog.

15

Abby fumbled for her cell phone where it sat on the bedside table and checked the time. Five-fifty Sunday morning. She groaned internally. Six days and her internal clock had already been corrupted. She could hear the patter of raindrops on the roof, and on the leaves outside the open window. The loons seemed to be enjoying the wet weather and were calling back and forth.

Max came around the end of the bed, having apparently heard Abby stirring. She stood looking at Abby for a moment, but then to Abby's surprise, the dog turned and headed out the bedroom door and Abby could hear her heading down the stairs to the basement.

Abby lay there for a moment, pondering the change in routine. No more wake up team. Yes! She could sleep in again. She took a deep breath and relaxed into her warm nest of blankets... and realized she was wide awake.

"No, no, no! Dammit!" *Just when the canine wake-up Nazi lets me stay in bed, I can't sleep.* Abby threw back the blankets and swung her legs out of bed, totally disgusted at this change in the status quo.

Ten minutes later, Abby was dressed and downstairs, staring out the kitchen window at wet landscape and wondering if the animals still ate in the rain. She figured they probably did. She heard Max coming up the basement stairs and turned to see her walk over to the kitchen door. The dog looked back at Abby, and again at the door, obviously waiting for Abby to open it for her.

"I guess a little wet weather doesn't stop you, does it Max." The dog glanced briefly back up at Abby as she reached for the doorknob and pulled the door open. Before Abby could stand back out of the way, Max brushed past, and trotted out into the steady rain. Abby stood on the porch and watched her progress. She stopped briefly on the edge of the woods to heed the call of nature, then moved along the blackberry and raspberry bushes that Gordon had planted in front of the trees, sniffing and squatting periodically.

"I guess that's the canine version of the morning news," Abby said to herself, turned and walked back into the kitchen. Cali Cat was sitting in the middle of the floor, washing her face, and ignoring Abby, the rain and the open door.

"I take it you're not a fan of the rain, huh," Abby said to the cat. Cali Cat didn't respond. She didn't even look at Abby. "Are you sure you don't want to go with your partner in crime?" Again no response. Abby walked over and reached down to stroke the cat's head, causing her to stand and arch her spine so that Abby's hand traveled the entire length of her back and tail. "At least you let me pet you. You might want to talk to the canine component of this household. Let her know I'm not such a bad person?" Not even a meow served as a response, and the cat wandered off, apparently intent on spending the day somewhere warm and dry.

"I guess there's no sense in putting it off any longer," Abby said to herself. A waterproof jacket hung on a coat rack next to the door. Abby slipped it on over her uncle's fleece, and pulled on a pair of his rubber wellington boots which were only a little too big. Tying the hood tight under her chin, she headed out the door and into the rain.

The remainder of the day was spent under an unending blanket of clouds and drizzling rain interspersed with periods of intense downpours. Abby found she was mesmerized by the wet weather, probably because days like this so seldom happened in Phoenix, and when it did, if felt like a gift from God.

As it turned out, native Michiganders didn't feel quite the same way about the rain as she did. Adam called fairly early to see if she'd had any problems with the chores. She had to admit she felt pretty proud of herself when she informed him that all the chores were finished, and Autumn, the goat, hadn't tipped over the milk bucket even once.

Adam laughed and congratulated her on her accomplishments, then hung up after reminding her that dinner was at 6:30, but to feel free to come over any time before that.

Dishes done and floor swept, Abby sat savoring her second cup of coffee when the phone rang. Expecting it to be Lucy, she eagerly picked up the receiver.

"Hey Luce. How are you doing there in warm sunny Phoenix? You wouldn't believe the kind of weather we're getting today."

Silence met her on the other end of the line.

"Luce?"

"Hey Abby? It's me again." Josh's voice came over the line.

"Dammit Josh. We went through this the other day. I told you not to call me anymore!

"Abby, I really think you want to reconsider." Josh's voice took on a soft menace that Abby had never heard before. It chilled her more than anything she'd ever heard come out of his mouth. Even those times when he'd threated harm to himself or her, there was more of the tone of desperation than of threat.

"Josh, I have absolutely no intention of reconsidering. I never want to talk with you again. In fact, I intend to block all of your calls in the future so that I don't have to. I'm hanging up now, and don't call back." Abby slammed the receiver back down on its hook, and made a mental note to buy a phone with caller ID the next time she was in town and maybe see if the phone plan for the house could be changed so that she could block specific numbers. She was more and more convinced that Josh had finally gone around the bend and the farther she was away from him, the safer she would stay. She had enough things on her plate right now with trying to find out who killed her uncle without Josh complicating things.

The phone rang again, and Abby snatched it off the wall so angrily that the entire cradle pulled off its anchor and the whole thing went crashing to the floor.

"Josh, I said leave me alone!"

She started fumbling to pick up the phone cradle so that she could hang up when she heard, "Okay, but I'm not Josh."

Abby collapsed into a nearby chair, and put the phone back to her ear. "Hey Lucy. Sorry. I didn't realize it was you."

"That was pretty obvious, Abb. Josh hasn't given up yet, huh?"

"No, he hasn't. I'll have to call Rick on Monday and see if there's any way to get a restraining order put on him from here. At the very least I'm getting caller ID and blocking him from all my social media.

"Making your way slowly back into the twenty-first century, I see. Do I take it that you've decided to stay? After all, a new phone is a pretty big commitment," Lucy said.

"I... I think I'm leaning that way, Lucy. I guess I'll decide for sure once I've finished figuring out what happened to my uncle."

The two talked for a few more minutes as Abby told Lucy about her visit to Sommerfield's office and what she'd unearthed while there.

"You know, Abby, your friend Adam is right. You need to be careful if someone truly killed your uncle."

Abby sighed. "Yes, I know Lucy. You don't have to remind me. But all I'm going to do is a little research online so that when I go to Deputy Morrison, I've got something that will convince him to investigate. Nothing will happen if I'm just punching a few computer keys, unless it's a case of carpel tunnel."

"Yeah, if you stop there, which knowing you, Ms. Closer, is not likely to happen."

Abby laughed at the use of her old nickname at Daniels Advertising. Her coworkers considered her to be doggedly persistent in bringing in and retaining clients and Lucy's use of the term in this situation felt like it was swinging awfully close to the truth.

"I'll keep my nose clean, Lucy. Don't worry. Right now the biggest concern I have is the best way to set up and advertise my business, get an email address for the fish farm, and maybe start a website. It took almost all day yesterday to find a place in the house where I could get adequate reception for the Wi-Fi hotspot so that I could get the computer on line. Oh, and I have to go to Adam's for dinner tonight."

"Is this the 'your uncle was like a dad to me' Adam? Is something brewing in that direction?"

"God, you've got a one track mind, Lucy! No. Nothing is brewing. Adam's more like a brother, and he's got an absolutely wonderful girlfriend named Jenn who lives with him. No, his mother is coming over. Apparently she drives over from a nearby town every week or so to see him, and as she liked Gordon and was grateful to him for all he did for Adam when he was injured in the war, she wanted to meet me as well."

"Uh huh. Sounds totally plausible." Lucy's skepticism was palpable.

"I mean it, Lucy. There's nothing between Adam and me."

"Oh, I believe you. What I don't believe is that Adam's mother just wants to thank you. If your uncle and Adam were as close as you say, then maybe she is thinking Adam should have inherited the farm over someone who has never even been in the vicinity of a pile of cow poop. What better way to correct the situation than to see her son marry the heir and get the farm that way."

Abby was so shocked she couldn't think of anything to say and just sat looking dumbly at the receiver as though it had grown ears and a tail.

"Hey, Abby, are you there? Can you hear me?"

"Uh, yeah." Abby coughed, clearing her throat. "Yeah, I heard you. You did hear me say that Adam has a girlfriend didn't you? There's no way he'd date me to get the farm... geez doesn't that sound like some trashy bodice-ripper novel? You know *The Farmer's Daughter*... well niece."

"He may have never thought of it, or have any intention of marrying you, and you may have no intention of marrying him, but do you even know what his mother might think? Does she like his girlfriend?"

"No, as a matter of fact. Adam said she doesn't like Jenn at all. But she didn't like Jenn before Gordon had his accident, so there's no way that has anything to do with him getting the farm. In fact Jenn said that Gracie doesn't like her because she can't have children."

"Oh." Lucy drew the syllable out longer than Abby thought possible. "Even more of a reason to want her son to dump Jenn and start seeing you. You have the farm her son should have had, and a functional uterus."

"Just be quiet for heaven's sake, Lucy!" Abby was torn between outrage and laughter. "I am nervous enough about meeting this woman. Adam said he thought she had designs on Gordon herself. Now there's no way I'm going to be able to look her in the face."

"Oh, you'll figure things out. Just be careful what you

eat while you're there. Who knows, she might try and knock you off in hopes that Adam would be next in line to inherit. Maybe a little cyanide in the soup?"

"Enough already!" Abby was laughing harder now. "First you have her plotting to get rid of Jenn in favor of me, now you have her killing me in favor of Jenn! I have to sit down to dinner with this woman and make intelligent conversation, and all I'm going to be able to see is some crooked crone stirring her pot and muttering incantations. There's no way I can pull this off!"

"Okay, I'll stop. I need to get off the phone anyway. I want to get out and run some errands before it gets any hotter. Ah, the joys of Phoenix in the summertime. Take it easy Abby. Please be careful when you're researching these developers. Big money can earn big enemies."

"Don't worry Luce. I told you, I'm just looking up information on the computer to give it to the sheriff's department. They won't even know what I'm doing, and I'm not going anywhere near these investors."

"Just like you didn't go anywhere near Sommerfield, right? Just be careful. Gotta run now. Talk to you later."

"Take care of yourself in the heat."

"Will do... take care of yourself with the soup."

"Shut up!"

Laughter met Abby's ears as the phone clicked, indicating the end of the phone call.

16

Abby choked and started coughing, causing the others at the table to look at her with concern. She grabbed her glass of water and took several swallows, trying to clear her throat.

"Are you okay, dear?" Gracie Thomas, Adam's mother, asked with a worried look on her face.

"Uh, yes, thank you. Something just went down the wrong way." Abby used her napkin to dab her eyes which were tearing from the exertion of trying to expel errant saliva from her trachea. "What was it that you were saying?"

"I just asked if you would like some mushroom soup. I got the recipe from a neighbor. Apparently her grandmother brought it with her from Poland shortly after World War II when they immigrated and settled in this area. She said that it was best made with wild mushrooms. But you always have to be so careful that wild ones aren't poisonous, so I went with store bought." The older woman smiled gently at Abby, but in her mind's eye she saw the lanky, white-haired woman bent over the pot, stirring and cackling maniacally.

Abby looked at the loaded plate in front of her wondering how on earth she was going to make it through all that food. An empty bowl sat to the right of the plate, and Gracie had a ladle hovering over the bowl, and a pot of soup in her oven-mitted hand. Abby looked up and saw Adam looking at her with a grin on his face. Jenn, sitting to her left, was studying her plate, her golden blonde hair obscuring her face, but Abby could swear a small smile lurked around her lips.

"I guess. Just a little though. Everything looks so wonderful I'm afraid I'm going to explode if I eat it all."

"Nonsense," Gracie said, spooning two large ladlesfull of soup into the waiting bowl. I'm sure that you don't eat enough, you're so thin."

"I..."

"Mom, enough. Stop pestering her. Now sit and eat your own dinner."

"Fine, Adam." Gracie carried the pot of soup back into the small kitchen of the double wide, and pulled off the oven mitt and set it on the counter as she walked back to the table and slid into her empty seat.

"How was your day, Abby?" Jenn asked as she cut a small piece of her steak.

"It was very... quiet I guess. Peaceful. I got a lot of things done." Abby pushed her hair, which she'd worn loose that evening, back over her shoulders.

"I spent most of yesterday setting up a home office in the second upstairs bedroom. There was some old furniture stashed in the barn, and I was able to rescue a few things." She crinkled her nose at the memory of dust and spiders.

"Now that I'm back online, I spent the day getting things set up for a business. I've got an email and a Facebook page for the fish farm. I'm debating on a website, but I'm not sure it's worth it for such a small operation."

"It sounds like you're planning on moving to the farm then, Abby?" Gracie paused with her fork halfway to her mouth.

"Well, yes, I'm leaning in that direction. I've been thinking of opening my own business for a while now, and this may be the best opportunity... if I can keep my computer working correctly. My reception still seems to go in and out a bit. I may have to go with a dish."

"What is it that you do?"

"I worked for an advertising agency in Phoenix, but I've thought of opening a business that focuses on marketing and website design as well as social media."

"That's fascinating, isn't it Adam? I'm sure you'll do well here. I take it you have no boyfriend or husband that will be moving here with you?" It was Adam's turn to start coughing, and Abby became worried that someone was going to have to perform the Heimlich before he caught his breath.

"Are you all right, Adam?" Gracie looked at her son with concern.

"Yeah, I'm fine. Maybe you're getting a bit personal, Mom?"

"I'm sure Abby doesn't mind if I'm interested in her, do you Abby?"

Abby was uncomfortable with Gracie's focus on her, and even more uncomfortable with how the older woman completely ignored Jenn's existence, but she wasn't exactly sure how to drive things in a more favorable direction. Deciding that avoidance was the best policy, she jumped into a completely different topic of discussion.

"Hey Adam, I did some research on that company that created the development plan for Loon Echo Estates. Turns out that the drawing was commissioned by something called LEE Development, LLC, and since it's a limited liability company, it's registered with the state and that information is public record."

Adam frowned and set his fork on the edge of his plate.

"Abby, I thought you promised that you were going to turn everything over to Morrison, and stay out of the situation."

"I'm not in the situation. I just did some research. I want to make sure that when I talk to Morrison, I've got enough information that he's going to want to open the investigation again and not just tell me that I'm imagining things."

A crash of glass startled Abby. She, Adam and Jenn all turned as one to stare at Gracie who was mopping spilled water off the table with her napkin. "I'm so sorry Adam, Abby... Jenn. My fingers slipped. I guess that comes with old age." Gracie seemed unaccountably flustered. "Excuse me a second, I need a bigger towel." She picked up her plate, which had been flooded when she dropped the water glass she'd been holding.

Jenn started to push her chair back, "Let me help you, Gracie."

"No, no. I've got it, thank you Jenn."

Jenn settled back into her chair, but looked as though a spring would pop her up again at any point, like a jack in the box, and Abby wondered how many more twists it would take until she exploded.

Gracie returned from the kitchen carrying a dish towel with which she quickly cleaned up the remainder of the spill. She returned the towel to the kitchen, and came back with a clean plate and a second glass full of water.

"Please, don't let me keep interrupting the conversation. Do I understand correctly that you think someone killed your uncle?" Gracie still showed slight signs of the agitation that Abby saw after she dropped the water glass, although for the most part she'd regained her composure.

"Yes, I do. I don't believe that my uncle would have started drinking again, at least not to the point that he would have been so drunk as to fall into the water and drown."

"You know, I thought very highly of your uncle. He and I spent a lot of time together and I was heartbroken when he died." Abby watched the emotions flit across Gracie's bony face and started to feel a twist of sympathy for the lonely woman. Then out of the corner of her eye she saw Adam studying his plate as though all the mysteries of life were engraved upon it and remembered what he'd told her the other day about how his mother was pursuing Gordon, and how her uncle had felt about it, and she felt the sympathy start to wane slightly.

"So," Gracie continued, apparently unaware of the nonverbal conversation flying around the table, "what have you discovered so far? Who are these people you're looking into?"

Abby paused for a second, debating the wisdom of talking about her theories to a stranger, even though when it came down to it, everyone there was a stranger to her. Then she decided what could it hurt? It wasn't like Gracie was connected with LEE Development, LLC after all.

Quickly Abby filled Gracie in on what had happened at Sommerfield's office.

"Then Friday, at the farmer's market, I had Rick take a look at the pictures I shot of papers I found in that folder. He noticed that at the bottom of the map it listed LEE Development, LLC. He said they were likely the ones who had commissioned the drawing and the plan, although he also said it may have been more for advertising at that point, and not totally accurate as to elevation and fine detail.

"He thought that the planner who drew the map might have used a drone instead of actually surveying the land on the ground, which would have been trespassing. Apparently drone use is new enough that they're still determining what laws govern it, and it would be difficult to argue a trespass case in court just based on looking at empty land."

"What about them offering land for sale that they don't own?" Adam looked at her curiously.

Abby chewed her lip in concentration, a frown in her hazel eyes. "I hadn't thought of that. I would think that wouldn't be legal, but I'm not sure they're doing that.

The sign said 'coming soon' on it. That's a good question, though."

"What did you find out when you looked up this LEE Development LLC?" Gracie asked, studying her plate as she cut her food.

"William Sommerfield is listed as a member, unsurprisingly. So is a Theodore Archer from Alpena, Michigan and a Robert Lundgren of Rogers City."

"Ted Archer!" Adam exclaimed, taking Abby by surprise.

"Yes, that's what it said. Why? Do you know him?"

"No, I don't know him, do you Mom? Jenn?" Both of them shook their heads. "Ted Archer is the head of one of Alpena's old-time families... the ones who started the town and built its main industries. There've been rumors for years that the Archers have fallen on hard times, and it's only through the skin of their teeth that they've been able to keep the huge stone house out on the point down on the Thunder Bay shore. Ted owns one of the largest construction companies in the area, and they've built many of the residential, commercial and industrial structures in the area. The great recession hit them hard, however."

"Well, apparently he's one of the owners of LEE Development, LLC. I haven't gotten a chance to look him up yet, nor the other guy, since I spent so much of yesterday just to get the computer talking with the mobile hotspot and finding all the places where I don't get enough signal to get on line, and today I was busy with the business end of things."

"How much more information do you need?" Jenn asked, looking at Abby with concern in her bright blue eyes. "You're just giving the information to Morrison, and surely he'll have to do his own investigation."

Abby felt a small rock of stubbornness grow in her chest. "Yes, I know I'm giving everything to Morrison, as soon as he contacts me, but I'd still like to know something about these guys. Don't worry. I won't put myself in danger. Besides, I've got Max, the wonder dog, there to protect me. So, Adam, when do I have to order more baby fish?"

With that, conversation moved into safer territory, as far as Abby was concerned. Although, she did catch Gracie watching her several times during the dinner and Abby had the uncomfortable feeling that she was sizing up her uterus.

It was getting dark when Abby finally looked at the clock and realized it was after 8:30. "Adam, Jenn, I think I'm going to call it a night and head home. I still have some work I want to get done before bed."

"Do you want me to drive you back?" Adam asked.

"No, it looks like the rain has stayed away, and I'll enjoy the walk. There's still plenty of light out, and as long as Big Foot keeps his distance, everything will be fine. Gracie, thank you so much for inviting me. Dinner was great."

"It was wonderful to meet Gordon's niece. I heard so many wonderful things about you, I feel like I know you already," Adam's mother said, again giving Abby the disquieting feeling that the Gordon she was talking about was one who existed only in Gracie's mind. "I hope we'll get together again soon. I would love to see what you do with your uncle's bachelor den up there on the lake."

"Uh, sure. That sounds great." Abby turned and gave Jenn and Adam hugs and headed out the back door into the fresh air. Once the door shut behind her she took several large breaths, as if trying to dispel the cloying miasma emanating from Gracie Thomas. No wonder her uncle had tried to avoid the woman.

A tinkling-rattling sound from behind caused Abby to jump and turn. Max, who had walked up to Adam's house with her earlier in the evening had apparently chosen to curl up and sleep on the back porch while Abby was inside. As Abby stood there, Max rose and shook, the tags on her collar clattering together.

Earlier in the evening, after the day's rain had finally let up Abby was feeling a slight case of cabin fever, and decided to walk the short distance to Adam's home. At that time Max, predictably, had decided to walk with her, and had refused all arguments to the opposite. Finally Abby decided that Max knew the way well, having stayed with Adam after her uncle passed away, so it wasn't like she was in a strange place. Adam tried to get the dog to come into the house when Abby got there, but as soon as Max saw Gracie, she planted her feet and refused to budge. Abby begged, commanded and tried to trick her, but nothing worked. Ultimately Adam said to go ahead and let her stay outside, and she'd probably go back up to Gordon's house.

Abby felt a little shiver of satisfaction when she saw that Max had waited for her in spite of Gracie's presence and the absence of the Dakota.

"Are you ready, hound?" Abby called to Max as she walked up.

Max sat at her feet, and looked up at her, studying her face as though trying to determine if Abby had made it away from Gracie unscathed.

"I understand your feelings, Max, but we have to play nice. She is Adam's mother after all. Let's head home."

Abby started walking down the driveway with Max bounding ahead of her, then sniffing the ground and bounding back to Abby again, always making sure she was out of petting range. Still Abby felt like she'd made progress with the dog. After all, she had stuck around to protect her from Adam's mother.

17

Abby was sitting at the kitchen table, working on her second cup of coffee Monday morning when she heard a vehicle grumbling up the driveway. Rising, she walked to the window to see if Adam was coming up to check and see if she'd done the chores correctly. However, instead of Adam's red truck, she saw a white and blue SUV, emblazoned with the Presqe Isle Sheriff's Department logo. The driver steered the vehicle toward the house, and pulled to a stop next to the Dakota. The driver's door opened, and Abby saw Deputy Benjamin Morrison climb out into the light morning drizzle. He looked skyward, then pulled the collar of his jacket up to his ears and ran toward the back door of the house. A flurry of motion caught the corner of Abby's eye, and she turned her head to see Max run out of the barn, headed for the back door as well, apparently feeling she needed to keep an eye on the visitor.

Abby hurried over to the back door and opened it just as Morrison reached the stairs.

"Deputy Morrison, I wasn't expecting you. Please come in. Get out of the rain."

Morrison stepped onto the door mat and stomped his feet several times, knocking off mud and bark debris, then stepped up into the kitchen. Water dripped slowly off his jacket, and plastered his dark blond hair to his head. He heard the clatter of claws on the steps behind him and stepped aside to let Max run in, although she wasn't polite enough to knock the mud off her paws first.

"Max! Stop! Sit! Stay! Uhhh, you filthy dog!" Abby exclaimed in annoyance as Max slithered through the chair legs and under the kitchen table, laying where she could watch Morrison. The deputy looked momentarily startled, but regained his composure quickly.

"Good morning, Ms. Williams. How are you doing?" Morrison started to unzip his jacket, pulling it off his arms, and hanging it on the coat rack over a rubber mat. Checking his boots, and assuring himself that all the mud was gone, he stepped off the inside mat and onto the linoleum floor, putting out a hand to shake Abby's.

"I'm fine, Deputy Morrison." Abby found herself looking up into those intense blue eyes again. "But I'm surprised to see you. Please, call me Abby."

Morrison smiled and nodded at the invitation.

"You did leave me a message on Friday evening. I didn't receive it until yesterday, and thought I might as well stop by instead trying to take care of it over the phone. It sounded like you had some things you wanted to show me?"

"Uh, yes," Abby said flustered. "I have some things to tell you that I've discovered about my uncle's death, and a few things to show you as well. I guess I just wasn't expecting a personal visit."

"No worries. I have a few other situations to take care of in Onaway and it sounded like you had something you felt was pretty important." Abby thought that he sounded skeptical, but that he'd listen the same way he'd listen to any crazy old lady who thought there were terrorists hiding in her basement, ready to steal her cinnamon-raisin bread recipe and sell it to the highest bidder. Abby felt her hackles rise at being lumped into the conspiracy theorist group in his mind.

"Yes, well, why don't you come sit down and I'll show you what I've found out." Abby could feel the ice freeze over in her voice, and from the sudden blue ice look from Morrison, it appeared that he hadn't missed it either. Consciously trying to warm her tone she asked, "Can I get you a cup of coffee? It's pretty damp and chilly out this morning Deputy."

Morrison studied her for another moment.

"It's already made, it's not a problem, I..." Abby started to stutter, trying to cover her earlier gaff.

"I'd love a cup of coffee, Abby. I appreciate it." He moved over to the kitchen table, pulled out a chair and sat, watching her every move. "Please, call me Ben."

Damn, if it's not the dog watching me, it's the police. Abby went to the cabinet, pulled out a mug, and filled it from the pot. "Can I get you cream or sugar Deputy Morrison... uh Ben? Although the cream is actually goat's milk since I forgot cream at the store the other day. But the sugar is real sugar."

"Black is fine, thank you. If you don't mind, I'd like to see these things you think I'd be so interested in. I do have to get into Onaway, and you never know when a call might come in."

"Cow at large?" Abby joked, and immediately kicked herself since even she could see it sounded like she didn't think the sheriff's department capable of anything but animal nuisance calls.

"Maybe," Morrison responded. Then suddenly he grinned at Abby, and all the ice thawed in his eyes. "A month ago I got a call about a strawberry thief."

"That didn't happen, did it?"

"Yes, I'm not lying to you. A local berry grower was sure that his strawberries were being poached overnight. He even set out cameras, but hadn't managed to find the culprit. We figured that some local was sneaking in and picking at night in order to sell on the side of the road the next day." Abby stared at Morrison, mouth and eyes wide in shock... as much from the supposed crime as from the fact that he'd loosen up enough to tell her about it. "I sat out all night waiting for the criminal, only to find out that a huge family of raccoons was hitting that end of the field. It was surprising that we hadn't found tracks or half eaten berries, but there you go. I've now got the reputation in our admittedly small department as the guy who busted the great racoon caper."

Abby had started laughing as he described the raccoon raid. Morrison took a sip from his mug and looked pleased with himself.

"So, Abby, what is it that you think I should know?"

For the next few minutes Abby went over Sommerfield's visit to the house, and her visit to his office the following day. She pulled out the printouts of the photos she took which she'd made on the new printer. She then told him what she'd found out regarding LEE Development LLC.

During the entire recitation, Ben Morrison listened politely. He examined the photos carefully, taking a magnifying glass which Abby unearthed in the junk drawer to examine the legend at the bottom of the artist's rendering.

As Abby's story ground to a stop, she watched Ben's face. Several moments of silence followed as Ben continued to look through the papers, then look through them again. Finally he looked up at Abby, an expression of sympathy in his eyes, but his voice was calm and matter of fact.

"Do you have duplicates of these printouts? May I have these?"

Abby felt a thrill of hope that he believed her and was going to reopen the case.

"Yes, those are duplicates. You're welcome to take them. You're going to look into this, right... reopen the case? You can see that there's motive to kill my uncle."

"You've definitely uncovered some interesting information here, Abby. But I really don't know if it makes much of a difference. As you said, Mr. Sommerfield wasn't even in the state at the time of your uncle's death, and as we discussed before, it would have been risky killing Mr. Dorsey, as there was no guarantee that the heirs would want to make a deal. And, in fact, if I understand you correctly, that's exactly what happened. You, as the sole heir, intend to live on the farm, and have no intention of selling to Sommerfield, so if he or any of his partners had engineered your uncle's death, it was for nothing."

"But maybe they thought it was worth the risk since my uncle was adamant about not selling for development. Maybe I'm in danger. Maybe...," Abby stopped, frustrated and unsure what to say to convince Morrison to investigate.

"There are a lot of 'maybe's, Abby. Let me take this folder. I'll look through it, show it to my captain, maybe to the county attorney. See what they say, but I'll be honest, I don't see them agreeing to reopen the case. While some of this information may be probative, I just don't know if it's enough." Ben started to push his chair back to stand.

"I hope then you don't care if I keep looking into the situation," Abby said. Her earlier feeling of camaraderie over the raccoon story had evaporated in the mists of defeat.

Ben looked at Abby, a slight frown on his face. "As I told you before, you're going to do what you think you have to do. However, you should know that Sommerfield could lodge a complaint about the information you essentially stole from his office. Do not take your desire to prove your uncle was killed to the point that you are breaking laws that could wind up with you in jail."

Abby refused to meet Ben's blue eyes, knowing that she was on shaky ground legally with the pictures she'd taken while in Sommerfield's office.

"Do you understand, Abby?"

"Yes, Deputy Morrison. I get your meaning." She saw

Ben's look sharpen at her use of his title instead of his first name.

"That aside, if there is something to your suspicions, and mind you I don't believe there is, but if there is some validity, then you could theoretically put yourself in danger if you pursue this in the wrong manner. This really is something that you should leave to professionals."

Infuriated, Abby jumped to her feet and confronted Ben, angrily meeting his eyes in a challenge. "Then maybe the professionals should do a full investigation and I wouldn't feel the need to interfere."

"I'm sorry if I offended you, Ms. Williams. I assure you I will examine the information you gave me. I just don't want to be investigating two deaths."

With that, Ben gathered up his jacket and headed back out the door and into the damp day beyond. Abby followed him to the door, and watched as he splashed through the puddles to his SUV, climbed in, started the vehicle and pulled out. The entire time her mind whirled with things that she wished she'd said. The sound of claws on the linoleum heralded Max's emergence from under the kitchen table. She walked cautiously over to the kitchen door, and stood next to Abby, looking out into the rain as Ben headed out the driveway.

Abby shut the door, and looked down at Max. "You know if he thinks I'm going to stop looking into Gordon's death, he's got another thing coming." She felt more determined than ever, Morrison's condescending air serving to put fuel on the fire instead of water.

"So what do you think, Max? Are you in?"

The dog had been watching Abby's face intently as she spoke. A sharp bark answered the question, although Abby told herself it was probably just because the dog heard her name.

"Fine. It looks like it's just the two of us. The first thing I need to do is call Ted Archer, and convince him that I'm the best web designer money can buy, and he needs to meet with me.

18

The secretary at Archer Construction informed Abby that Mr. Archer was tied up for the remainder of the day, but that he had an appointment available on Tuesday at 10:30 if she'd like to meet with him. Abby replied in the affirmative and hung up. She debated on calling Robert Lundgren and making an appointment with him as well, but eventually decided that it would be best to poke one hornets' nest at a time.

The internet search the day before disclosed that Robert Lundgren was a civil engineer and community planner based out of Rogers City. His Linked-In profile listed several developments which he'd designed in the lower part of the state, but not much else. She did find a rudimentary website which showed examples of his work. Abby studied the pictures which showed both artist's renderings and actual photographs of beautifully laid out subdivisions. Nowhere was Loon Echo Estates mentioned, and she couldn't find the large drawing she'd seen in Sommerfield's office. Nothing on the website or the Linked-In profile shouted "murder" to her, although truth be told, neither did anything she learned about Archer.

Abby spent the remainder of the day developing a business plan. She told herself that this wasn't because she had absolutely decided to stay, but just in case...

In her searches she determined that there were a number of small advertising agencies and printers in the area, but with the way the industry was growing these days, and the changes in technology, a designer didn't have to live anywhere near her customers, as long as they didn't feel the need for frequent face to face meetings, and were willing to communicate via phone, video conferencing or email. She was sure that at least a few of her long time clients in Phoenix would continue to use her, even if she left Daniels Advertising. In fact, a couple of them had been hinting at her going it on her own for several years, unhappy with some of the changes that had been happening in the firm.

She was sitting at the kitchen table working on a logo for her business card and brochure when the phone rang making her jump. Quickly jotting on a nearby piece of paper she was using as a shopping list "Phone w/ caller ID," she picked up the receiver and said hello, praying that it wasn't Josh again.

Instead of his deep baritone voice, a slightly nasally female voice responded.

"Hello, Abby?" Confused, Abby looked at the receiver as though she could see down the line to whomever was at the other end. Who knew she was here, and knew her number? It wasn't Lucy or Jenn.

"Yes, this is Abigail Williams."

"Abby, this is Gracie Thomas, Adam's mother?"

"Oh, uh, yes. Hi Gracie. What can I do for you?

"I just wanted to tell you how much I enjoyed meeting you yesterday, and I hope we can get together again in the near future." *Oh good God!* thought Abby. *Now that my uncle is gone, she's going to start chasing me.* Still, Abby didn't have the heart to be rude to the older woman who was obviously lonely and looking for friends.

"I had a good time, Gracie. I appreciate your inviting me."

"I was also hoping that you'd keep me in the loop on your investigation into your uncle's death. I hope those terrible developers who want to tear up Gordon's farm are caught and pay for what they did."

There was a strange note in Gracie's voice which made Abby uncomfortable, and she wanted nothing more than to tell her that the outcome of the investigation was none of the old woman's business. She tried hard to crush that feeling and muster the threads of sympathy she'd felt earlier.

"Gracie, I appreciate your concern, but I am only doing a little bit of calling around. Ben, uh, Deputy Morrison was here this morning and he doesn't think that there's a lot that he's going to be able to do, but he's going to be the one who does the investigating."

"Oh, I thought from the discussion last night that you were planning on pursuing the matter."

"As I said, I'm just doing a bit of calling around, and some internet searches. I'm not a detective, and I don't want to get in the way of the professionals." Abby felt a twinge of guilt at the irony of her using Ben's phrasing when he cautioned her. "The best I can do is keep things active."

"I understand, Abby, and I'm sure you're right. After all, I wouldn't want you to put yourself in danger's way. Your uncle wouldn't want that at all."

Again, a strange note in Gracie's voice made Abby squirm and she found she couldn't wait to get off the phone with the woman. She definitely needed caller ID!

"I'm sorry, Gracie, but I need to go now. I've got an interview tomorrow, and a lot of preparation to do to get ready since I didn't bring my portfolio with me. So if you'll excuse me..."

"Oh, yes, dear. Good luck with the interview. It was nice talking with you." With that Gracie hung up the phone and Abby was left looking at the receiver and wondering what all that was really about.

19

There is not enough caffeine in the world, Abby thought as she worked her way through the chores Tuesday morning. Even worse in Abby's book, was that Max was being an incurable morning dog, and for some reason had decided to stick close to Abby's heels the entire time. The dog's boundless energy seemed to suck what little Abby had right out of her body.

The day before Abby worked late scrabbling together a rudimentary electronic portfolio since the flash drive with her regular portfolio was sitting in her apartment in Phoenix. Then, for the first time since arriving at the farm, sleep eluded her. Her mind warred over obsessing on her meeting with Archer the next day, and anxiety over the changes she was planning for her life. Ultimately no problems were solved, but when the alarm chimed at 5:30, she'd still had fewer than three full hours of sleep.

Two hours later, chores done, showered and sufficiently caffeinated, Abby was starting to feel human and capable of facing the day with, if not enthusiasm, at least consciousness. She planned on heading into Alpena for her appointment with Archer early so that she could stop by the local copy store and run off enough business cards and brochures to get by for a short time. She figured she could order more online as soon as she was sure about what she was going to do, but she had to have something to hand to Archer today if she was going to convince him she was looking for his business.

At eight o'clock, Abby packed her computer, her business materials, and Max into the Dakota and headed for Alpena, She prayed Adam wouldn't be out in the workshop as she drove by his house since she didn't want to lie to him about where she was going. Abby told herself she wasn't actually breaking her word to Adam and Jenn. She was truly looking for business and who better to approach than the owner of one of the largest construction companies in the area Any entrepreneur in her position would do the same thing. Even Max didn't believe her arguments if the responding mutters and judgmental stares were anything to go by.

He wasn't in sight, however, and his truck wasn't in front of the house, so Abby figured he was probably out on a call and she was safe. Still she caught herself holding her breath until she was out on the county road, and heading in the opposite direction from Millersburg at sixty miles per hour. Even then she found herself tensing every time she saw a vehicle in the distance until she was sure that it wasn't Adam coming toward her.

Other than the fear of running into someone who would call her on her behavior, the drive into Alpena went easily. She remembered all the myriad turns, and didn't get any unexpected grand tours. Being a farming area, pocked with a multitude of small towns, most of them marked by nothing more than a church and a gas station, there were, according to Adam, many different ways to get from the farm near Millersburg to Alpena. That morning, however, Abby wasn't as much interested in exploration as she was in getting into town with time to prepare for her meeting.

She made a quick visit to a small copy shop she'd seen when she and Adam went to the farmer's market. Not twenty minutes later she walked out carrying a small stack of business cars and brochures. Examining them critically in the bright sunlight, she acknowledged that they weren't quite the quality she wanted, but they should do to get her in to talk with Archer.

At 10:15 Abby drove up to the huge old brick building in downtown Alpena that housed Archer Construction. She went through the now familiar routine of rolling down the windows for Max, gathered her materials and, taking a deep breath, walked to the huge double glass doors leading into the spacious front lobby. A small, dark-haired woman looked up from where she sat behind the large mahogany desk.

"Hello, can I help you?"

Abby hitched her bag up on her shoulder and approached the desk. "Hi. I'm Abigail Williams. I have a 10:30 appointment with Mr. Archer. I'm a little early."

"Oh yes, Ms. Williams. If you don't mind having a seat, I'll let Mr. Archer know you're here." The woman gestured to a line of comfortable looking chairs along the right hand wall and picked up a phone and punched a few numbers on the keypad.

"Thank you, I...," but the woman was already talking into the receiver. Abby walked over to the chairs, and sat as instructed. She looked around the airy room. It reminded her of Sommerfield's office, and she wondered if Archer and the real estate agent used the same decorator... one focused on tans, and pictures of buildings. Here, however, the pictures lining the walls were of some of Archer's more ambitious projects.

Over at the desk the phone buzzed, and the secretary lifted the receiver to her ear. Abby heard a murmured, "Yes, I will," and a few more words that eluded Abby's hearing.

The woman hung up the phone and turned to Abby. "Mr. Archer is available now, if you want to go through those doors." She indicated the double wooden doors to the left of the desk.

Abby stood and picked up her bag. Taking a deep breath, she marched determinedly across the lobby, opened the large wooden door and stepped into an equally roomy office. Stopping just inside the threshold, she looked around the room, and her eyes finally rested on the tall, muscular man sitting at a table desk on the far side under a large bay window.

"Hello, Mr. Archer? I'm Abigail Williams with LEE Web Design and Marketing."

At Abby's mention of LEE, a slight frown crossed Archer's face and his gaze sharpened. Abby held out a business card which Archer received warily, as though it were going to explode.

"It's a pleasure to meet you Ms. Williams. I'm told you want to talk to me about my web site?"

"Actually, Mr. Archer..."

"Please call me Ted. May I call you Abigail?" The cautious regard of a few moments before dissolved into a warm smile and Abby found herself responding with one of her own.

"Abby, please. As I was saying, I'd actually like to talk to you about all of your advertising needs. I've just moved to the area, and was looking through the websites and information available on some of the local businesses, and yours was one of the ones which stood out for me."

Archer's smile became rueful. "I take it that it stood out because it needs a bit of help?"

"Uh," Abby was so taken by surprise that she momentarily was at a loss for words. Finally she decided to go for broke.

"Yes, as a matter of fact. From what I've read, your family has been in this area for generations. Your ancestors helped build this town, and you have a lot of history here... a solid foundation so to speak," Abby smiled, encouraging Archer to enjoy the word play... a builder having a strong foundation. "But your website doesn't utilize that, and frankly it's a bit dated. There are a number of typos on it, and the photographic work is substandard."

Archer was nodding throughout Abby's presentation. "Thank you for your honest appraisal of the situation, Abby. I agree wholeheartedly. A while ago the young man we were using for our website, as well as all our advertising, went out of business and disappeared. It was quite a mess, as this guy had all the passwords and somehow tangled everything up to the point I just didn't have the patience or skills to untangle it.

"Laura, my assistant, was able to start a rudimentary site, but she doesn't really have the flair, or the time, to give the job the attention it needs, given her other duties. She's been after me to find a new person, but I've been a bit occupied with other things."

"If you like, Ted, I can show you some samples of sites I've worked on, give you some references, and can discuss what your company needs, what I can offer and..."

"And what it would cost?" Archer grinned at her.

Blast! Abby thought *I like him. I don't want to believe he killed Gordon.* Abby found herself responding to Archer's cheerful, matter-of-fact style, and found that she really hoped that she'd get his business... Business that wouldn't exist if he was a killer.

The guy she really wanted to be guilty was Sommerfield. In her book, murderers should always be annoying blowhards that made everyone shrivel in disgust. It would make life so much easier.

"Okay, Ted. Let me pull out my computer, and we'll go over some samples... and prices, and see what we can do about putting together a package that works for you." Abby smiled, trying to push down the feelings of conflict.

The two of them had been working for approximately an hour, lining out the direction they wanted the website to take, the features which Archer thought were important, and additional ideas and suggestions from Abby to make the site distinctive. Archer had a library of old photographs from Alpena's early days, and buildings that his father, grandfather and great-grandfather had helped build, and Abby was already envisioning a "foundation" themed site that emphasized quality over time.

The two were discussing the particulars of the contract when a sudden banging on the door made both of them jump.

"What the..." Archer started to rise, but before he could get more than halfway out of his chair the door was thrown open with a crash. Bill Sommerfield strode into the room and pointed at Abby furiously.

"What is she doing here?"

"Giving me a quote on a new website, and some other excellent advertising ideas, if you must know," Archer said mildly as he finished rising to his feet. "How are you doing, Bill. Did we have an appointment?"

"You know she accused me of murder, right?"

"Yes, you called me right afterward if I remember correctly." Archer's tone and expression were both bland.

Shocked, Abby stared at Archer, then Sommerfield, and then back at Archer. "You knew who I was when I came in?"

Archer looked to where Abby was sitting in the chair next to him. "I didn't know the minute you walked in, no. I'm not sure Bill here used your full name when he called to complain. I figured it out, although when you said the name of your business... LEE Web Design and Marketing? Subtle."

Abby and Sommerfield both spoke at the same time, making what each other said unintelligible. Archer held up his hands. "Stop. I didn't understand any of that. Now, ladies first. No Bill, wait your turn." This last was said as Sommerfield started to sputter in protest.

Abby felt as though she'd fallen down a rabbit hole and had popped out in some strange new world where she didn't know the rules. She looked briefly at Sommerfield, then back to Archer. "Why did you meet with me then, if you knew who I was?"

"I need a new website, and advertising agency."

"You're doing business with her?" Sommerfield broke in. His face was turning a decidedly unhealthy shade of red under the silver hair, and Abby began to worry that he was going to drop dead of a stroke before she got to the bottom of what was going on.

"That's what my contract says, and I tend to believe contracts."

"Do you realize she sent the sheriff's department to talk with me and accuse me of killing her uncle?"

"I believe you mentioned that when you called last night as well as just now when you came in, although I'd prefer not to get repetitive. I agree, that could be disturbing." Archer turned to Abby who was watching the two men, trying to figure out what was happening. "Abby, I believe Bill informed you that he was in another state at the time of your uncle's death."

"Yes, he did. But I also know that there is a lot of money involved here, and that LEE Development LLC had proceeded with things like a plat, and a rendering, even though my uncle would never agree to sell his farm for something like your development. There is a motive for any of you. How do I know you didn't all work together to kill my uncle and cover it up?"

Archer nodded his head in understanding. "Yes, we would stand to make quite a nice profit if we'd been able to either partner with your uncle, or buy his property from him, but honestly, it's not enough to commit murder."

"It is if your company is on shaky ground, and I've heard that Archer Construction fell on hard times." Abby felt a growing sense of frustration.

"Yes, the housing and construction crash in 2008 was tough on my business, as well as on Bill's and on Robert's, but the economy is rebounding, and at least in my case, I've got plenty of business. It's one of the reasons I want to make sure I have a good website and advertising person."

Abby's chin jutted up at a stubborn angle. "Okay, if it wasn't worth killing for, then where were you when my uncle died?"

"You can't be serious, Archer? You don't mean to let her get away with this interrogation, do you?" Sommerfield spluttered. Abby thought she could see his blood pressure rising as she watched.

"Yes, I intend to set this to rest, once and for all." Archer turned from Sommerfield back to Abby. "I believe from the news reports I read, your uncle was found in the lake in the morning of August second, and he'd been seen alive at approximately six-fifteen the night before by his tenant. Is that correct?"

Abby nodded, feeling numb.

"Well, during the first two weeks of August I was involved in several sailboat races, so most of the time I was out of town, and those nights I was in Alpena, my wife will verify that I was home with her by seven every night. There's no way I could have made it from Millersburg back to my house in less than an hour." Archer reached over for his phone, and started to punch in some numbers. "Do you want to talk to my wife?"

It was then that the farcical nature of the whole conversation hit Abby and she was torn between laughter and tears.

"No, please Ted. I believe you," Abby said.

"Great. I'd hate for my web designer to think I was a murderer." Archer smiled at Abby, inviting her to share in the joke.

"Wait a minute, you still intend to hire this woman?" Sommerfield blustered.

"Yes, Bill. I'm a realist. She's not going to sell us the

land around Lake Ellen. When you think about it, I don't blame her for thinking that one of us might have had something to do with her uncle's death. And, I need a good marketing person."

"But the time and the money we invested!"

"You and Robert made a decision to invest time and money into a project that wasn't a sure thing. My opinion is that we need to write off that money as a loss and move on. Abby, are you satisfied that neither I nor Bill could have killed your uncle?"

"Yes, I guess so, but....," that rabbit hole kept getting deeper and deeper.

"But you haven't met Robert yet."

"No, I haven't. He's the one who did the artist's rendering and the layout of the development. He's obviously got time wrapped up into the project."

"You're right, he does. Maybe not as much as Bill here," Archer gestured at Sommerfield who had collapsed into a large armchair, finally beyond speech. Abby examined him surreptitiously, trying to determine if they needed to call 911 to treat him for either a stroke, a heart attack or a nervous breakdown. The last seemed the most likely at this point.

"I suppose I could call and set up a meeting for you, but I'm really not sure that it would be successful. I would think that your greatest asset in investigating your uncle's death would be the element of surprise, and you pretty much lost that after visiting Bill."

"I suppose that's true," Abby grudgingly admitted.

"Good. I suppose I can expect a visit from the sheriff's department or their counterparts here in Alpena, as can Robert, but other than that, I imagine we're about done with issue, and can move forward. Bill, do you have any other concerns you'd like to address to Abby?"

Some incoherent mumbling emanated from the seated form.

"Wonderful." Archer took Abby's hand. "Abby, I look forward to doing business with you, both from an advertising standpoint, as well as trying some of that delicious trout I hear you raise on that farm of yours. If you don't mind, though, I do have another appointment I must get to, so if you'll excuse me?"

With that, Archer turned away and started packing a briefcase. Feeling as though she'd just been dismissed from the king's presence, Abby slipped her computer and papers into her bag and headed out the double doors into the lobby. On her way by, she glanced down at Sommerfield, who was at that point sitting, staring into the distance and not making a sound.

Laura, Archer's assistant, was once again sitting at the large reception desk typing on the computer, referring occasionally to several handwritten sheets at her side. She looked up as Abby walked by.

"You're leaving? Well, I'm sure we'll be seeing you again soon." She gave Abby a bright smile. "You don't know how happy I am that you're taking over this website and advertising stuff!"

Abby returned Laura's smile with one of her own. The last surreal hour had just given way to normalcy again. "I'm looking forward to it. I'll be in touch."

With that, Abby headed out the front door, aiming for the truck and a return to sanity. Then Max's head popped into sight in the driver's seat of the Dakota, and she realized that she might never see sanity again.

20

Over the majority of the drive toward Millersburg Abby replayed the scene with Archer and Sommerfield in her mind. She tried to pick holes in their alibis. As much as she liked Ted, and wanted to work with him, she also realized that didn't necessarily mean that he wasn't a killer. She just didn't want him to be. She sort of wanted Sommerfield to be, since he still rubbed her the wrong way, but just as liking someone didn't make him innocent, disliking someone didn't make him guilty.

"But how do I get around the fact that Archer was sitting on a sailboat in the middle of Lake Huron? And how about Sommerfield sitting in a lodge in Colorado?" Abby said to herself.

Max lifted her head from the tightly wound doughnut that she'd curled herself into on the passenger seat and studied Abby's face.

"So, do you have any suggestions?"

Max answered with a soft woof, then a couple of syllables of what Abby had come to call "yodelese;" those rising and falling sounds that were somewhere between a soft howl and a bark.

"Okay, so I have to cross Archer and Sommerfield off the list. It still could be Lundgren, although Archer's right that I've lost the element of surprise as far as he's concerned. Maybe I could get Adam or Jenn to help me."

Max sneezed, which seemed to be her general response

to things she thought were too foolish to be dignified with an actual answer.

"You're right. They're against this whole thing. They'd never agree to..."

It suddenly hit Abby that she was discussing strategy with a dog. A few moments passed in silence as Abby considered the situation. She finally decided to heck with it. If she wanted to discuss things with a dog, that was her business, and besides, no one could see her in the car, right?

"So, Watson, who is on the list of suspects if it's not Sommerfield or Archer?"

Max uttered another soft chuffing sound.

"Robert Lundgren, who stands to lose as much money as the other two. And, he's put time into the drawings and the surveying. Maybe some of the local farmers who don't want the land sold and developed." Abby chewed her lip for a moment, thinking.

"There was Jake Solinski, the guy who fixed the flat. He seemed to want to avoid my questions. But you liked him. You even let him pet you." Abby glanced at Max, once again feeling miffed that she still hadn't been able to touch her own dog. "You wouldn't let someone who killed Gordon pet you, right?"

A sharp bark answered Abby's question and she glanced quickly back over at Max who had risen back to a sitting position.

"Well," Abby said grudgingly, "I guess it wouldn't make much sense for a local farmer to have killed him, since the odds were that the heir or heirs would sell the property, and Archer and his cronies would likely be able to outbid anyone else since they stood to make the most money off the land and an heir would be more likely to go for a big payout instead of taking less money to leave the farm a farm."

A thought forced its way to the top of Abby's mind. It was a thought that had snuck in several times, and Abby had always pushed it back down. Adam.

No! Not Adam. Just like with the farmers, Adam wouldn't have benefitted from Gordon's death. In fact, he would have likely lost his home if the heir... if she had sold the farm. Could he have been so angry at Gordon, who facing cancer and not living much longer, had still insisted on giving the farm to someone who wouldn't love it as he would, that he'd have killed her uncle in a rage?

No, from everything she had learned about Adam in the last few days, she was sure that he genuinely loved her uncle, and would never have harmed him, even in a fit of rage.

That brought her back to Lundgren, and the impossibility of her visiting him and getting any information since both Sommerfield and Archer would have likely warned him in advance. Would they have done it already?

"Max, how about you and I take a trip into Rogers City instead of heading home?"

Max pointed her nose into the air, pursed her doggy lips and uttered a long string of syllables, looked at Abby intently, then curled back up in the passenger seat, resting her head on her hindquarters.

A small smile tweaked Abby's lips. "I'll take that as a yes."

When Abby reached Hawks, she turned right, instead of taking the left that would lead her to Millersburg, and from there to her farm. While she couldn't remember the location of Lundgren's office exactly, she knew from her previous trip that the closer she drew to Rogers City, the greater her phone's reception would be, and she had no doubt she could look up his address again. It was still early afternoon on a Tuesday, so, Abby reasoned, he would likely be in. Maybe not available, but at least around.

Also, hopefully, since Archer and Sommerfield were both under the impression that she'd dropped her investigation of LEE Development LLC after she'd been outed earlier in the day, maybe they wouldn't have bothered to fill him in yet, other than he might be expecting, or have already gotten a visit from Deputy Morrison.

Abby navigated her way through the streets of Rogers City down to Lake Street and searched for an open parking spot. Even though it was the end of August, Michigan's law prohibiting the start of school until after Labor Day meant that there were still a number of families out, getting in one last trip before the school year started. Considering that in most of Arizona, the schools had been in session for at least a month, it was strange to see children out of the classroom at this time of day on a Tuesday.

Abby finally found a spot and pulled in and looked

at Max who had awakened once they entered the small streets of the town.

"Okay, girl. I'll be back in a little while. If you don't hear from me in an hour, come looking, got it?"

Abby got a woof in return for her quasi facetious comment. There were times, she thought, that she really thought the dog understood every word she said.

And then there were the times she ate horse poop.

Lundgren Consultants' office was on the second floor two blocks down from where Abby parked. Located in an old walk-up building it boasted an amazing view of Lake Huron, liberally dotted with sailboats on this beautiful late summer day. Several times while walking down to Lundgren's building Abby paused and stared out at the lake, listening to the seagulls and watching the white caps roll in to shore.

She had to hand it to Lundgren. Even if he was a murderer, he had great taste in location.

Abby reached the red brick structure that housed Lundgren's office. The ground floor was taken up with an antique shop, the front bay windows filled with collectibles and pieces of art. On the northernmost corner of the building there was a white painted door that lead to a narrow staircase by which one could access the second floor and the four professional offices located there. Reading a plaque next to the door it appeared that Lundgren shared the space with an attorney, an interior decorator and an accountant. Lundgren's office was 2A, which, when Abby reached the top of the tall stairway, was at the southern front corner of the building.

She knocked on the wood and frosted glass door, then tried the knob, and finding it open walked into the small, shabby room. A large light table sat against the far wall, flanked by loaded bookshelves. The only thing in the room that looked modern was the large wrap-around desk, with a state-of-the-art computer, gigantic monitor, and laser printer.

A tall, lanky man, with thin dark hair was sitting behind the computer, completely engrossed in whatever was on the screen. However, at Abby's entrance he looked up, then pushed his chair back from the desk and stood.

"Yes, can I help you?"

"Are you Robert Lundgren?" Abby asked, momentarily sure that she'd come into the wrong office. This man didn't strike her as the type who would enjoy hiking around in the outdoors and planning developments. If it weren't for the light table, she'd have figured she got the accountant's office by accident.

"Yes. And you are?"

"I'm Abigail Williams. I think you've probably heard of me?"

Lundgren looked at her quizzically, tipping his head to one side and then the other, reminding Abby of Max. The dog did the same thing whenever Abby talked to her. She almost expected the man to start barking at her.

"Ah, no. I don't believe so. Did you leave a message? I'm sorry; my answering machine has been acting up lately." The man gestured to a cordless handset on an answering machine base sitting next to the computer.

"No, Mr. Lundgren. I thought maybe Ted Archer or Bill Sommerfield would have called you about me. I'm Gordon Dorsey's niece. I inherited his farm after he passed away."

Lundgren took on a distant look, as though he were trying to place her uncle's name. Then, just as Abby was going to say something else, his gaze sharpened, and he looked at Abby with curiosity.

"Yes, I remember now. Bill Sommerfield approached me regarding the possibility of developing the land that is, or I suppose was, your uncle's farm. He called it Loon Echo Estates, in an attempt to woo down staters with the cute name."

"Yes, I saw a drawing that you did in Bill Sommerfield's office."

"That was my buy in on the company, or at least part of it. Keep in mind, I was the least of the three partners, and I debated long and hard before agreeing. I don't like to see developments popping up like zits on the landscape."

"Why did you do it then?"

"Bill is an old school friend of mine. He's always been pretty driven, if not the world's greatest personality. Still, I figured he'd get it done one way or the other, and I thought if I was part of the development, then hopefully I could design something that worked with the ecology of the area, versus wiping it out."

"You make it sound like you didn't really agree with developing the land around Lake Ellen." Abby was confused.

"Honestly, I'd have preferred it to remain a farm." Lundgren came around from behind the desk and perched on the edge while talking to Abby. He seemed completely at ease.

"Still people seem to gravitate toward these types of places. They see its beauty, want to have it for themselves, then destroy it in the owning."

Lundgren looked off in the distance for a moment, as if seeing the bulldozers move in and wipe out groves of trees. He shook his head slightly, sadly, then looked back at Abby.

"So, what can I do for you? If you've inherited your uncle's farm, are you now going to go into business with us?"

"No, actually I'm thinking of staying and keeping the farm up and running. I'm planning on starting my own web design and advertising company to supplement the income from the trout farm."

A sunny smile flashed across Lundgren's face.

"Excellent. I'm glad to hear it!" He stood up and came forward to shake Abby's hand.

Abby hesitated, then took his extended hand in hers, shaking it briefly.

"Won't that cost you money, though? I mean if I don't sell?"

"Well, it will of course have cost me the time I spent on the preliminary plans and the rendering, but like I said, I was the least of the partners. It will cost me some, but I have enough business to keep me busy."

Abby looked around the office, the slightly shabby condition of the walls and floors, the lack of comfortable chairs and other amenities for clients, and looked back at Lundgren, a question in her eyes.

"No, don't let the office fool you. I do much of my work out in the field, or through video conferencing." Lundgren gestured toward the corner and Abby could see that if clients were only exposed through the webcam, then they wouldn't realize how the rest of the office was decorated, or not decorated as the case may be.

"So, Ms. Williams, we come back to why you're here. What can I help you with if you're not planning on developing your land?"

"I..." Abby hesitated, and then rushed forward. "I came to see if you were the one who killed my uncle?"

The look of shock on Lundgren's face was comical to say the least. He choked, then started coughing and couldn't catch his breath.

I guess I got the element of surprise after all, Abby thought as she looked around the room for something that might help, wondering if she should call 911. Finally her eyes rested on a water cooler with several plastic cups sitting on a small table nearby. Grabbing one she filled it with cold water, then held it out to Lundgren who had started to get his coughing under control. He took several sips, cleared his throat, then took a few more. Finally he staggered back over to his chair and collapsed into it.

"Are you all right?" Abby asked, as she examined him critically.

"Uh, yes," Lundgren said in a froggy voice. He coughed a few more times, and took another sip of water. "Yes, I'm fine." His voice sounded stronger, and Abby began to think he might make it after all.

"Now let me get this right. You want to know if I killed your uncle? Why on earth would I do that? And, for that matter, why would I tell you if I had?"

"Well, you could have killed him in hopes that the heirs would sell the farm and you'd get a chance to see your development come to fruition. You might have wanted the money, which I'm told would be considerable."

"True, I would have made some money, but it wasn't enough to kill for, and I'd prefer to see the land remain undeveloped."

"Okay," Abby drew out the word to its utmost. "Well then, can you tell me where you were the night my uncle was killed?"

"Probably. When was it?"

"The second of August, around nine at night from what I'm told."

"Easy, I'm sure I was home, like every night. Probably watching the History Channel. Sorry, but I was alone. There's no one to vouch for me. You'd just have to take my word for it."

Abby was so frustrated she wanted to cry. Lundgren, apparently seeing her emotional state said quietly, "What makes you think your uncle was killed and not that he just had an accident? The way the news reported it, it sounded like a pretty open and shut case."

"There are reasons but I don't really want to go into them with... ah, with..."

"With one of the suspects?"

"Yes, exactly." Abby looked at Lundgren, as if daring him to contradict her decision.

"Well, Ms. Williams, I can tell you one thing. Anyone who went to your uncle's farm to hurt him would have had to deal with that dog of his. I've only been there once, when I was doing some aerial photography in order to develop a plan, and that shepherd heard me a half mile away and came tearing through the swamp to drive me off. I would say any stranger showing up on the place intending to do your uncle harm would be leaving with some bite marks."

Lundgren's comments hit Abby like a rock. He was right. She'd always assumed that whomever injured her uncle had also locked Max into the fish house. However, as Adam had pointed out earlier, Max wasn't likely to go for just anyone, and that refusal was likely to involve teeth. Besides, how on earth could Lundgren, or even Archer or Sommerfield, have known where the keys were to get into the fish house in the first place? She was so sure it had to be one of the members of LEE Development LLC that she'd totally ignored the canine component of the crime.

"I should have thought of that, Mr. Lundgren," said Abby, feeling completely disgusted with herself. *What kind of investigator am I ignoring inconvenient evidence.* "I appreciate your willingness to talk with me." She started to turn to leave.

"I hope you find what you're looking for Ms. Williams. Do call me if I can help you, but for what it's worth, I hope that you stay and keep the farm as a farm."

Abby nodded and walked toward the door, pausing as a thought struck her. She turned back to Lundgren. "I suppose I should warn you that Deputy Morrison might stop by to ask some questions. I gave him al the information I had on LEE Development LLC."

Lundgren grinned at her. "I'll look forward to the visit,

Ms. Williams, but I assure you that I'm an open book, and he can ask away."

Abby nodded again, and headed out into the hallway, closing the door quietly behind her. With every step closer to the street she felt a growing lump in her chest. She was so positive that LEE Development LLC was the key to her uncle's death. Now she wasn't so sure and she had no idea which direction to head next.

As Abby stepped out onto the sidewalk and turned to walk back to the truck, she heard someone call her name from the other direction. Turning she saw Deputy Morrison heading in her direction at a fast walk and the look on his face said he wasn't pleased.

Mustering a welcoming smile, Abby said, "Deputy Morrison... Ben, it's nice to see you."

"I wish I could say the same, Abby. May I ask what you're doing here?"

"I just wanted to talk to Robert Lundgren about LEE Development LLC, and his development plans." Abby could feel her chin going up in a defiant attitude, and she deliberately lowered it and adopted a more placating posture and tone. It wouldn't do much good if she continued to deliberately prod Morrison.

"I believe I said I would look into the situation."

"Not quite. What you actually said was that you'd talk to your captain and the county attorney about it." *Damn, that defiant tone again.* "I just wanted to know more about what was going on with this development, and Lundgren is a part of it. I heard you went to talk to Sommerfield."

"And I heard that you went to meet with Archer, and now I find you here." Morrison took a deep breath and looked around, noting the tourists walking past, staring at them. "I would prefer not to discuss this out here, however."

"Honestly, Deputy Morrison... ah Ben, I don't really see the point in discussing it at all. I just talked with

Lundgren, and I don't think he did anything to my uncle, although I might be wrong. I assume since you talked to Sommerfield and Archer, that you'll also be talking to Lundgren. He says he doesn't have an alibi," Abby said helpfully.

"I had intended on talking to him now, but I saw you coming out of the building and thought I'd discuss things with you first. I take it you've come to the conclusion that your uncle's accident was just that... an accident."

"No, I haven't decided that at all. I just don't know which direction to head next if none of the members of LEE Development LLC are involved. I'm no less convinced that my uncle's death wasn't just an accident."

Morrison rubbed his forehead with his right hand, as if trying to decide how to proceed. Finally he looked at Abby. "I'm going to talk to Lundgren for myself... you say he's in right now?"

"Yes, I told him you might be coming to see him."

Morrison looked at the sky, his jaw tightened for a moment, but when he looked back at Abby, his voice was calm. "I'm going to talk with Lundgren, and I'll go ahead and re-interview some of the other people I talked to at the time of your uncle's death, but I really don't think it will turn up anything new. However, things are slow right now, and my captain okayed a little time spent on this. But you have to face it Abby, you may never know exactly what happened that night."

"I'm sorry, Ben. Right now I just don't agree with you on that. There's an answer out there somewhere. Someone knows what happened. I appreciate you looking, however."

With that, Abby turned and headed down the sidewalk to where the truck was parked.

As she walked toward the Dakota she saw Max's head pop into view. Lundgren was right. There was no way Max would have allowed a stranger to lock her into the fish house without a fight, even if that person had a key. It had to be someone that Max knew, or they had to have disabled her somehow. That brought her back to Adam and Jenn, and her mind refused to visit that scenario. She trusted them.

There had to be another answer.

22

Adam's truck was in front of his shop when Abby turned in to the gravel driveway leading to the farm. On the way back from Rogers City, it dawned on Abby that she didn't know where her uncle's keys had been found after his death. She knew Adam had a key to the fish house, but who else had access to one, and would Max have trusted any of them enough to follow one up to the fish house and get locked inside?

It was nearly time for chores and Abby started to drive past the shop, then at the last moment pulled over to the large building and parked next to Adam's red pickup. As she opened the Dakota's door and started to get out, Adam came out of the shop to see who was there. Max, excited to see him, jumped out of the passenger side window and ran up, wagging her entire butt.

"Hey Max! How are you doing girl?" Adam squatted down to pet the dog, scratching her behind the ears and working his fingers into her ruff in a way she must have enjoyed, as the rear end began to wriggle even faster.

There's no way Max would let Adam touch her like that if he was the one who killed Gordon. Abby watched with a rueful smile on her face.

"You know she still won't even let me pet her on the head? I'm allowed to feed her, and that's about it. I'm getting a terrible inferiority complex here."

"Don't worry, Abby. It will come. She's already getting closer to you than she does to most women, and you've only known her a week. It took two months before Jenn could pet her."

Abby groaned. "Has it only been a week? It seems like I've been here half my life!"

"Grows on you fast, doesn't it? So what have you been up to today? How did your interview go? Mom called and said you had an interview with a potential client in Alpena."

"Uh...," Abby paused. She'd already broken her promise to Adam; the one where she'd vowed that she'd leave the investigating up to the sheriff's department. She didn't want to lie to him on top of that.

"It went well. At least I got the job."

"Hey that's great! I'd give you a hug, but I'm filthy. Come on into the shop while I finish up some things and tell me about it."

Abby followed Adam into the cavernous workshop, and saw a huge tractor which appeared to be broken down into in several very dirty pieces. A large slab of metal sat a few feet away on a bench.

"It looks like you're pretty busy. Maybe I ought to go. We can talk later." Abby leaned over and peered at the chunk of machinery.

"No, I'm done for the day. Jenn will be home shortly. I just need to clean up a bit." Adam picked a rag out of a pile and started to wipe his hands, then headed for a deep utility sink at the back of the shop. "So who was this interview with? What will you be doing."

"It looks like I'll be doing all the web design and advertising materials for...," Abby paused, then taking a deep breath continued, "... for Archer Construction."

The words fell like lead in the room. Adam looked at Abby with a frown on his face. "I thought we agreed you'd leave the investigation to the professionals."

"I know Adam. I just wanted to meet this guy, see what he was like. I'm alive and safe, aren't I, and I even have some new business to show for it," Abby said brightly, trying to gloss over the fact that she'd done exactly what she'd promised not to do.

"What if he'd known who you were?" Adam was visibly upset. He wadded the rag up and threw it toward the bench, but it fell short and landed on the floor a few feet from Abby. Looking for something to do, and reluctant to say what she knew needed to come next, she stepped forward and picked up the material and started to fold it.

"Don't bother. Just throw it in the laundry bin over there. It's got grease all over it. Don't get it on your clothes." Adam's voice was harsher than she'd ever heard it. "Well, what if he'd found out?"

"If you must know, he knew who I was when I walked in."

"What! He knew you were Gordon's niece? I thought you said you got his business?"

"I did. I'm as surprised as you are. He knew who I was, and he said it didn't matter. He did say that he was on a sailboat race when Gordon died, or at home with his wife, and he offered to let me speak with her to verify his alibi."

"That had to have been an interesting conversation."

"Honestly, he seemed to think it was something of a joke. Sommerfield was livid, though." Abby kept twisting the cloth in her hands, looked down and realized that black grease was coating her fingers. "Do you have another one of these?" She threw the dirty rag in the bin Adam had indicated.

"Yeah, over there." Adam indicated a stack of rags at the end of the bench. Abby walked over and picked up the top one and started trying to clean the black grime from her fingers.

"Sommerfield showed up? What was he doing there?"

Abby stared down at her hands, focusing on the grease and the rag to avoid looking Adam in the eyes.

"He showed up to complain to Archer that Deputy

Morrison had questioned him on his whereabouts at the time of my uncle's death, and about LEE Development LLC."

"Wow, sounds like you opened a can of worms. I take it he wasn't too happy?"

Abby shook her head, light brown pony tail bobbing from shoulder to shoulder.

"No. He was pretty explosive, but Archer got him under control. Archer didn't even seem to mind that the police would be talking to him, either. I don't think he did it."

"Okay, so now you've ruled out two of the three. I think that..." Adam noticed an expression on Abby's face. "Don't tell me. You've met the third guy... Lundgren... too?"

"Yeah, I had time on the way home, so I went to Rogers City to meet him before the others had the chance to fill him in." Abby chewed her lip.

"And?"

"And, I don't think he did it either, although he doesn't have an alibi like the other two." Abby made a move to throw the rag into the laundry bin as well, then stopped and examined it more closely.

"Hey Adam, what is this rag?"

"What?" Adam looked confused at the abrupt change in topic. "I don't know. It's just a rag. Whenever we get old clothes, you know shirts, jeans, anything really, that can't be worn anymore we tear them up and make them into shop rags. Believe me; I go through a lot of rags. Why?"

Abby ran her fingers over the dark green flannel scrap. "Max carried up a piece like this from the lake the other day. She shoved it at me and I thought she wanted to play fetch, but when I threw it she went and got it, brought it back, but refused to release it again until..." Abby paused realizing how silly the next part would sound.

"Until what?" Adam looked curious.

"Well, until I told her I wouldn't throw it again," Abby said with a sheepish expression on her face.

Adam burst into laughter.

"Yeah, well you can laugh. You're not the one living with the canine Einstein are you?"

"Oh, don't worry. She's made a fool out of me a number of times."

"It's curious, though. I mean that you have some of the same material in your shop?" Abby held up the rag and saw it was a roughly torn square.

"Probably not that strange when you think about it. I'm always up at Gordon's and he was always down here. I imagine that at some point he grabbed a rag for something and stuck it in his pocket. Either that, or I had it in my pocket at some point when I went up there and I either took it out for something, or it fell out."

"Maybe, but what Max found was an entire sleeve, ripped loose at the seams, not a nice square like this one."

Adam frowned. "What are you saying Abby? Why does it matter where this piece of material came from?"

"When I was talking to Lundgren, he mentioned that the one time he came out in order to get some areal pictures, Max heard him and came tearing down to chase him away. He also said he bet that anyone who tried to lock Max into the fish house would come away with some injuries, unless of course Max knew that person very well. What if she grabbed his sleeve and tore it loose?"

"Abby, I don't like what you're saying. Are you accusing me of killing Gordon?" The pained look on Adam's face broke her heart.

"I... No, Adam! I don't think you killed Gordon. Even by accident. I know you wouldn't do anything to hurt him."

"I hope so." The cold fury in Adam's voice froze Abby. For the first time since meeting him, Abby saw the well of anger... the potential for violence.

"Adam. I don't suspect you. Please. I just think that this material has to have some meaning. Could you find out where it came from? Please, Adam."

"Abby, I'm sorry. I really think it would be best if you went home now. I'll see what I can find out about the rag, but right now I think it would be best if you weren't here."

Adam turned his back on her and walked out of the shop, heading for the house.

"Adam! Please stop."

Adam paused for a second, then without turning he said. "Not right now Abby. I know you're just trying to find answers, but I can't deal with this right now."

Adam walked to the back door of the house, opened it, and disappeared inside, leaving Abby standing in the doorway to the shop alone staring after him.

Max ran partway to the house, following Adam, then stopped and looked back at Abby. She hesitated, one front foot in the air, as if about to take another step, then she whirled and headed back the way she'd come. When she reached Abby, she sat and a stream of barks and yodeling emerged like none Abby had ever heard. Abby felt as though Max was chewing her out for upsetting Adam.

"I'm sorry, Max. I really am. I don't think Adam did anything to Gordon. I just... I just want to know what happened." Abby turned and headed for the truck, head down and completely dejected. Max followed close at her heels, but instead of jumping in the driver's door as she usually did when Abby held it open, she went around to the passenger side, and leaped in through the window.

Feeling as though she had just received the final snub of the day, she started the truck and headed the short distance to the farm, wondering if she'd destroyed any chance she had of making this new life work.

23

Chores that evening were done in a melancholy silence. Adam had told her a few days ago that they always tested the pH and hardness of the water on Tuesdays and Fridays as long as the weather wasn't too warm. They tested more often in hot weather, although they'd never had a problem. The artesian well pumped out water at a constant rate and temperature making a small trout farm like this one fairly easy to maintain.

The problem was, however, that she had no idea how to test the water, and couldn't remember from the previous Friday what the reading was even supposed to be. She guessed that another day wouldn't matter too much, as it had been relatively cool, and the fish looked healthy to her, thick speckled bodies flashing here and there in the water of the pond. Hopefully Adam would have forgiven her by tomorrow, and come help her with the water testing.

After finishing feeding all the animals, Abby found herself at loose ends, not wanting to go into the house, but not sure what to do outside. She considered calling Lucy, but a look at her cell phone told her that Lucy would still be at work. Dratted three hour time difference! While she wanted badly to talk to Adam, she also realized that she needed to give him some time.

As she stood indecisive in the middle of the driveway, she heard a flurry of loon calls. Over the past week she'd heard several different types of vocalizations from the loons, and had seen the large black and white birds at a distance. They never seemed to sleep, as she'd wake at times during the night to their yodeling.

She made up her mind and started for the lake, Max trailing along behind her. Gordon had both a kayak and a canoe, and while she'd never actually been in either, she'd seen videos and she was sure it couldn't be too hard. She was going to check out the loons. After all, if LEE Development LLC thought loons were important enough to name a development after, they had to be something. There had to be a good reason they didn't name it Duck Quack Estates.

The old grayed dock jutted out into the lake just down the hill from the house. On the bank, well up from the shore line was the small shed where Adam said the paddles, oars and life vests, as well as an assortment of fishing gear were kept. Abby searched through her jean's pocket for the ring that held all of her uncle's keys. She looked through the assortment, trying to figure out what opened what.

There was the house key, the truck key, the small round-topped brass key to the fish house, and three other silver keys, similar in size to the brass one. Adam had told her he didn't know exactly what each key went to, except for the one to the fish house, the truck and the house. In his opinion, Gordon hadn't known exactly what each went to either, having forgotten to take them off his ring when a padlock broke or got lost. Abby had laughed at that, especially when Adam recommended hanging on to them for a period, but that at some point when she'd been there awhile, to either take them off and throw them away, or stick them in the "key can."

"What's the 'key can'?" she had asked, confused.

"It's where Gordon puts all the keys that have lost their locks. He's afraid to throw them away in case he comes across a lock he's forgotten about, but he also doesn't want to keep them on his ring and carry them around. So he puts them in an old coffee can."

When Abby went searching later, she came across the can, half filled with old keys. Her uncle must have lost a lot of locks.

Now she looked at the ring, and selected one of the silver keys, fit it into the padlock on the door of the boat house and tried to turn it to no avail. Next key, same response, and the next. Finally she looked at the brass key to the fish house.

"I know this goes to the fish house." She stood looking at the key, then over to Max who had wandered out on the dock and was looking over the edge, presumably at the schools of small fish that lived there. Abby had noticed them before when she'd come down to the lake to sit on the dock and dip her feet in the water.

Finally she decided what the heck, and fitted the brass key into the lock. She tried to turn it, not expecting much, and was pleasantly surprised when the key turned smoothly, resulting in a click and the shackle popped loose. That was nice, Abby thought, her uncle had the two locks keyed the same. Maybe he thought it would solve the "key can" problem.

She pulled the lock loose, pulled the bolt back, and hung the opened lock in the hasp. Opening the door she peered into the gloomy interior. A sound from behind made her jump and turn, only to see that Max had abandoned her fish watching and had come to look in the boat house with her.

The space was small and cramped, only about six feet by twelve, although fairly neat. On the right hand wall hung three single-bladed wooden paddles for the canoe and a long, double-bladed kayak paddle with white fiberglass blades and a black shaft. Deciding that the smaller vessel would be easier to handle, she pulled the kayak paddle off the wall then looked around for a life vest. She only saw one item that looked remotely like it was what she wanted. A floppy, y-shaped piece of nylon with various straps attached, obviously meant to fit over someone's neck and chest. A cord with a yellow plastic tag dangled from the bottom. She picked it up and examined it more closely. The tag identified it as a personal flotation device, but one that only inflated if the cord was pulled, releasing a CO2 cartridge.

Abby looked at the life vest for a moment, wondering if something like that truly worked. She looked around the shed again but saw no other more traditional life vests. Throwing the lightweight nylon over her shoulder, she turned and headed back out of the boathouse.

As Abby stepped out of the shed, Max brushed past her legs, actually touching her for a moment with her silky soft fur and Abby turned, thinking that the dog was finally going to allow petting. Instead, she saw Max rooting in a pile of ropes that were stacked on the floor beneath the canoe paddles.

Great, I was a road block not a reward. Abby sighed. She knew that it would take time. Everyone said so. But dang, she was tired of being rejected by the dog.

"Come on Max. I want to shut the door."

Suddenly Max jumped backward with something in her mouth, and came trotting toward Abby.

"Oh, no you don't! Not again!" Abby let go of the door and scooted backward, trying to see what was in the dog's mouth before it got shoved into her leg. Max hesitated, then came forward again more slowly and sat a short distance in front of Abby. In her mouth was another glove which she deposited at Abby's feet.

Abby set down the paddle and vest, and picked up the glove, with Max watching intently as usual. She turned it in her hands, examining it carefully, trying to determine what it was about the gloves that fascinated Max so much.

This glove appeared to be a mate to the first, although this one was cleaner, having apparently been left in the shed instead of the barn. She could tell this one was small as well, and also stiff from being wet sometime in the past. Several dark brown stains covered the palm and cuff, but other than that the light yellow brown of the leather shown through, unlike the filthy item Max brought her earlier in the week.

"Dog, you're giving me a headache," Abby said, exasperated. There had to be something about the gloves and the piece of material that made Max want to bring them to her, but she just couldn't figure out what it was.

Well, there's enough time to figure it out later. Abby started to jam the glove into her back pocket, then decided it would make too large of a lump to sit comfortably.

"I'm going to leave this in the shed, Max. I'm not throwing it away, okay?"

She headed back into the shed and set the glove on a small shelf nailed to the back wall. As she turned and started to walk back out of the boat house, Max pushed in and grabbed the blade of one of the wooden canoe paddles in her teeth. She started to back up, causing it to pull loose from its hanger and crash to the ground. Immediately the dog started dragging it out of shed by the blade.

"Max, I'm going out in the kayak, not the canoe. What are you doing? You're going to put tooth marks in the wood!" Abby went after the dog and paddle, trying to reach the narrow shaft. Max tried to turn, but the paddle caught momentarily in the doorway. Abby stooped to grab the shaft before Max was able to loosen it from where it was jammed.

The two engaged in a momentary tug-of-war, but it appeared that the wide flat blade of the paddle didn't offer as much purchase for a dog's teeth as the long thin shaft did for a human hand, and Max lost her tooth-hold.

Losing her balance at the abrupt change in momentum, Abby took a step backward and flailed her arms, losing her own hold on the paddle in the process. Max immediately grabbed the shaft of the paddle near the top, and pulled it out the door.

"Dammit, Max. Leave it alone!" She stepped out the door and reached again for the paddle, but this time Max pulled backward and the blade swung toward Abby, nearly hitting her in the shins. She skipped out of the way, then stepped down on the throat of the paddle, stopping its movement and forcing the shaft and grip down at the same time. Even at the increasingly awkward angle Max refused to release her hold on the shaft just below the grip, going down to her chest to maintain her bite.

Keeping her foot on the throat, Abby squatted down and grasped the shaft, then stood pulling the paddle up with her. At that point, Max, apparently having an advanced degree in leverage, ran to the right, causing the entire paddle to twist in Abby's hand, and swinging the blade toward her face. She grabbed the shaft with her other hand, and wrenched it backward, pulling it from the dog's mouth.

"Max! Knock it off! What's gotten into you?" Abby stood there, breathing hard, holding the paddle in both hands, ready for whatever Max's next move.

Instead of continuing the battle, Max backed up and started barking frantically, interspersed with periods of her own form of language.

Abby began to feel real concern that something was seriously wrong with Max. Did dogs have nervous breakdowns?

Abby rested the grip of the paddle on the ground, and squatted, holding onto the shaft for support.

"Max? Max, are you okay?" Abby said as soothingly as possible. "What's going on girl?"

Max's barking and howling tuned down to muttering and she lay down in the pine duff, intelligent eyes never wavering, her stumpy tail stirring the soft ground cover as it wagged furiously back and forth.

Finally Abby shook her head, not sure what to make of the dog's wild behavior and stood, using the paddle as a support, her knees popping in the process.

"Okay, Max. I really don't know what you're trying to tell me, or what's going on, but I'm going to put this paddle back in the shed now and..." As Abby rose to full height, her face moved past the blade of the paddle and something tickled her nose. She brushed her face, thinking a strand of her hair had worked itself loose from her pony tail. Then she saw something that made her heart stop for a moment.

The paddle was older, and the varnish was beginning to peel along the edge. In several places the wood itself was beginning to crack, one as long as two to three inches in length, and in that crack were five or six short, light brown hairs.

Abby froze and stared at the paddle for a moment, then rose the rest of the way to her feet, never taking her eyes off the hair in case it should disappear. She examined the edge of the paddle intently. No other cracks bore evidence of contact with something hairy. She glanced at Max who was still lying several feet away, watching Abby's every move.

"Okay, think rationally," Abby told herself. Max raised her head and barked once. Where could this hair have come from?

Max? No wrong color, even if the length was right.

One of the farm animals, the horses or the cows? Wrong length and texture. This hair was a light brown, fine and silky, and only a few inches long.

"It's human hair," Abby said softly. "It has to be human hair. But whose?" She felt torn between wanting to believe she found a clue that could lead to her uncle's death and afraid it was another red herring.

Adam's hair was dark brown, nearly black, and kept very short. It wasn't his for sure. Jenn's was blonde, Rick's curly and dark brown. Sommerfield's hair was silver, Archer's was extremely short, and Lundgren's dark brown. In fact, the only person on the place who had hair this color other than Gordon was Abby herself, but this was the first time that she'd been in the boat house. Beside, her hair was much longer than those few strands caught in the end of the paddle.

It had to be Gordon's hair.

Abby studied the paddle even more closely, but nothing else jumped out at her. She hesitated then suddenly turned and headed back up the hill toward the house, carrying the paddle carefully in front of her, terrified that the hairs would blow lose and she would lose all proof that they existed in the first place. Max scrambled to her feet and followed Abby closely as if also afraid that Abby would lose her find.

Once back in the kitchen, Abby set the paddle carefully on the table, went to the junk drawer, and looked for the magnifying glass that Morrison had used the other day. Feeling slightly Sherlock-ish, and completely foolish, she used the lens to examine the crack and the wood around it.

Under the greater magnification, Abby could see a difference in the color of the wood exposed by the crack. The upper part, that section closest to the edge of the paddle, was dark and weathered, as though the fissure had existed for a while. However, at the deepest point of the crack where the hair was trapped, the wood was lighter in color and looked newly exposed. Abby turned the paddle over and ran the glass over it, focusing so intensely that the rest of the world disappeared for a few moments. She was on the verge of stepping back when she saw it... in the edge of the cracked varnish. It looked like dirt, accumulated over time, but something about it caught her attention. She looked more closely at the dark substance. It was dark, red-brown. Her chest tightened. It looked like dried blood in a place that no dried blood should be.

Abby set the glass down on the table slowly, stepped back from the table and looked at the paddle, lying there so innocently. She looked over to where Max lay, joined now by Cali Cat who seemed determined to pull the dog's attention from Abby, rubbing back and forth under Max's chin, fluffy tail curling around the dog's nose. Max's attention never shifted from Abby. She shook her head when the cat's tail tickled her nose, but her eyes never wavered.

"You know what this means, Max?"

A soft woof answered her. No argument this time.

"Maybe we've got evidence. Maybe if not evidence of who killed Gordon, then evidence at least that it wasn't just an accident. Someone must have hit him with that paddle hard enough to knock him into the water. Maybe even struck him hard enough to make him pass out. That's where that head wound came from, not from hitting his head on the dock.

Suddenly Abby felt starved for oxygen and she realized she'd been so tense that her breathing was shallow. She took a deep breath, then went to the drawer where her uncle kept the plastic bags. She rummaged through the drawer and found several extra-large zippered seal storage bags which she'd seen earlier. She pulled one out and slid it carefully over the blade of the paddle, zipping up the closure until it was snug to the shaft. Then, feeling sheepish, but unwilling to take chances, she wrapped her hand in a thin bag that looked like it held fruit at some point in the past, picked up the paddle and placed it carefully in an empty corner of the broom cabinet. She knew that she and Max's earlier wrestling match would have likely destroyed any fingerprint or other DNA evidence left on the paddle, but just in case, she didn't want to do any more damage.

Paddle safely stored, Abby turned and looked at the dog. If she were honest with herself, she was a little freaked out. She may have joked with Morrison that she thought Max was possibly a higher form of life... an alien in dog's clothes, and while that was still a joke, she now wondered exactly how smart Max was.

"You smelled Gordon's blood on the paddle, right Max?"

A soft chuffing sound.

"Maybe you also smelled the person who hit him as well, right?"

Another soft woof.

"That person locked you in the fish house didn't he? That's why you don't like his smell and you went after the paddle?"

Max lifted her nose and her now familiar yodeling came out.

"I've got to call Morrison and let him know. He's got to get out here and pick up the paddle and get it tested."

Abby headed for the phone, picked up the receiver and punched in the Presque Isle Sheriff's Department's non-emergency number, then waited for the dispatcher to answer.

Two rings. Three. Then a deep male voice came on the line.

"Presque Isle Sheriff's Department, how can I help you?"

"Is Deputy Benjamin Morrison available? This is Abigail Williams."

"Deputy Morrison is off duty until Thursday. I can transfer you to his voice mail if you like."

Abby hesitated. Should she ask for someone else?

"Ms. Williams?"

"Ah... yes, that would be fine. Thank you so much." It had already been weeks, and the paddle was safe in the broom closet. Waiting until Thursday wouldn't matter.

Several clicks sounded over the line, and Morrison's voice came on, asking the caller to leave a detailed message and a phone number where he or she could be reached.

"Deputy Morrison, this is Abigail Williams. I found something today... ah... something that might have evidence on it that would prove who killed my uncle. A paddle with hair and I think blood. It was locked in the boat house. If you could give me a call as soon as you can I'd appreciate it. The number is..."

A beep sounded, cutting off the rest of Abby's message. She briefly considered calling back, but finally decided it didn't matter. He knew her number and where she lived. She didn't look forward to telling him how she found the hair in the paddle, but at least she had a little bit of time to get used to the idea.

A sudden flurry of movement and a crash caused her to jump, and she whirled toward where Max had been laying a few moments earlier. Apparently Max had gotten bored, and Cali Cat and finally enticed her into a wrestling match of another type. A kitchen chair was laying on its side, and the two animals looked at Abby guiltily.

Yeah, explaining to Ben that my dog is a genius and cracked the case is going to be easy. Abby shook her head, then picked up the chair and pushed it back under the table.

24

Abby was just finishing the morning chores when she heard a vehicle drive up outside the barn. She felt a flush of joy wash through her. Adam must have forgiven her and was ready to talk. Putting down the milk bucket, Abby hurried out of the room and to the front of the barn.

Instead of Adam's red pickup, Jenn's old green Jeep sat in front of the barn, and Jenn herself was getting out of the driver's seat. The spot of relief that filled Abby's chest a moment before froze and became dread. She peered through the dirty, bug spattered windshield to see if Adam was in the passenger seat, and just hadn't gotten out yet. No one was there.

Max ran out of the barn from behind Abby and up to Jenn who ruffled the dog's ears in greeting.

"Hi Max. How are you this morning?" Jenn looked up and saw Abby and a bright smile lit her face.

The knot of unease loosened. If Adam were still furious with her, surely Jenn wouldn't be showing up so happy and welcoming. Surely as Adam's girlfriend, she'd stand behind him, and be angry at Abby as well. Surely...

Amidst all the turmoil swirling in Abby's brain, Jenn walked up, apparently unaware of Abby's mental gymnastics and unconcerned.

"Hey Abby. Morning. How's it going?"

"Uh, good morning, Jenn. Things are going great, I guess. At least the goat thinks so. She got loose from the milk stand when I was getting more grain and drank half of the morning's output before I could stop her," Abby said wryly, rolling her eyes.

Jenn started laughing. "That sounds like Autumn. She loves her milk. Of course, she'll probably get the runs now, but you'll get more milk than normal this evening."

"Adam said I should get a dairy calf to help use up the milk now that the other calves are off it and none of the other goats need it at the moment. I don't know how to go about getting one, though."

"Oh, Adam knows several dairy farmers in the area. He can reach out to a few of them and they'll call the next time they have a bull calf. Adam will go with you, help you find a good one. Speaking of Adam, though, he asked me to come up and talk with you before I headed into town."

Abby looked at Jenn, then off into the pasture where the cows were grazing peacefully. At least she said that Adam would go with her to get a calf, so he must not be sending Jenn to deliver the message that they were leaving.

Abby looked back at Jenn. "I know he was pretty upset yesterday. Honestly, I don't suspect him of hurting Gordon. I know Adam wouldn't have done anything to him."

"Adam knows that, Abby. It just hit him yesterday, you asking about the rags like that, and when it comes down to it, how much do you actually know about us? We really just met a little over a week ago. I heard him talking to Gracie about it last night. Naturally her being gung ho behind him actually made him rethink his actions. It seems to work that way a lot." Jenn laughed, her eyes sparkling. "I figure her hating me is the best thing for our relationship sometimes."

"There's something strange with that sleeve being the same material as Adam's rags, but that doesn't mean I think he did anything. Like Adam said, Gordon could have picked up the rag and brought it back here, or Adam could have. Maybe it was left intact for a reason. I don't suppose you know where those rags came from do you?"

"Honestly, no. Most of his shop rags come from clothes that have gotten too old and trashed to use as clothes anymore, so I cut them up and throw them in the rag bag."

"Did he have a shirt like that? Or did Gordon?"

"No, not that I remember, but sometimes we get rags elsewhere, like clothes dropped off at the shop without an owner. Sometimes people are just cleaning out their closets, and want to get rid of things, but they're not good enough for me to sell them at the shop." Jenn shrugged. "Sometimes Gracie brings things she clears out. It's taken her a long time to go through all of Adam's father's things." Jenn took on a faraway look as though trying to pinpoint a memory that was tickling the edge of her mind. Finally she shook her head and took a deep breath.

"Adam wanted to talk to you himself this morning, but an emergency call came in from a farm over by Harrisville. A broken down combine that is desperately needed in the fields. On his way out the door he asked that I come up and let you know he'll come over later today or tomorrow sometime, and to tell you he's gotten 'over himself,' as he likes to put it." Jenn grinned at Abby, inviting her in on the joke.

Abby grinned back. "Well, I'll be glad to see him, and you of course. As a matter of fact, I've got some exciting news for you both. I may have found evidence, or Max has, if I have to be honest. A paddle with hair and blood. I think maybe that wound on my uncle's head wasn't from hitting the dock when he fell, but from someone hitting him with the paddle and knocking him into the water."

"Abby, that's fantastic. Have you called Morrison?" Jenn looked excited.

"I left a message for him, but he's out until Thursday.

I figured it wasn't really an emergency, so I just put it in a safe spot where any evidence won't get damaged... well any more damaged than Max and I already did by wrestling over the darned thing," Abby said ruefully, rubbing an up and coming bruise on her forearm.

Jenn laughed, her blue eyes sparkling. "I can hardly wait to hear this story, but I've got to get into town and open the shop. I've got to meet a new potential consignor at nine."

"You'd better get going then," Abby said, glancing at her cell. "Why don't you come up this evening and I'll tell you the whole story. I'll even cook."

"We'd love to, Abby, but we'd made plans to go into Rogers City tonight. One of Adam's best customers gave him a gift certificate to a restaurant in town, and we've been waiting to use it until things got settled here. Rain check?"

"You better believe it!" Abby nodded, brown ponytail bobbing. "Tomorrow then. Come up, and I'll give you the whole story. By then I should have talked to Morrison and will know whether this paddle is anything or not."

"Sounds wonderful. I'll let Adam know. I know he's been antsy about not getting the pH checked on the water, but it can wait until tomorrow I'm sure, as long as the fish are looking well."

"As far as I can tell they're fine. No one is packing his suitcase and moving to the lake at any rate. No one is belly up, if that actually happens. We'll plan on tomorrow then."

"Gordon's system is pretty stable from everything I hear. Still, it's not good to go too long and have a big problem creep up on you. We'll see you tomorrow."

Jenn climbed back into the Jeep and pulled out of the barnyard, waving as she headed down the drive. Abby returned the wave, then turned and headed back into the barn, wondering to herself what someone did with a goat with the runs.

The rest of the day went smoothly as far as Abby was concerned. She began work on Archer's new website, making a list of things she would need from Laura in order to get something professional up and running as quickly as possible.

She also spent some time researching the farming and marketing of trout. If she was truly going to make this work, she needed to have the knowledge instead of always relying on others like Adam to take care of the business for her. She soon became immersed in all the minutia of raising fish successfully, and by the time she emerged at chore time her head was spinning, and she wondered if she could ever learn everything she needed to know to make a go of this business her uncle had left her.

Chores were becoming more and more automatic, and she seldom had to consult the list she'd made of types or amounts of feed. Max followed her every move, never more than ten feet away. In fact, as Abby got thinking about it, Max had chosen to stay close to her all afternoon, whereas in the past she had usually disappeared off on her own business around the farm. Abby wondered what that meant, but looking at the dog, she decided it was likely she'd never understand Max's thought process. Maybe Abby smelt like bacon from this morning's breakfast, and Max was attracted to the scent. Maybe she thought Abby was going to steal the Dakota and head off into town without her. Who knew?

Regardless, as Abby finished chores and headed into the house for the evening, Max was right beside her, although as usual, just out of reach. The afternoon had gotten overcast, and a light drizzle of rain was starting again, making Abby feel chilled. While the house had central heating, Gordon had also installed a large black wood stove in the middle of the living room. Abby hadn't had the courage to tinker with it yet, but with evening fast approaching, and the weather looking to be chilly and damp, she decided to give it a go.

Fortunately for her, the internet held an wealth of information on how to start a fire in a wood stove, and the tin hod next to the stove held a wealth of logs. Next to that a large embossed tin box held what appeared to be a mixture of sawdust, lamp oil and paper. Just what she needed for tinder. Within ten minutes she had a large blaze roaring and the damp shivers were starting to give way to a warm toasty feeling. She picked up a light mystery that she'd been working her way through, and curled up in the soft suede recliner with Max and Cali Cat stretched out on the rug in front of the stove.

The three of them had been comfortably settled for about half an hour when suddenly Max lifted her head and looked toward the back of the house. Cali Cat, disturbed from her rapt kneading of Max's furry back, got to her feet, stretched languorously, then disappeared silently out of the room.

Abby noticed the movement and frowning, tried to determine what had caught the dog's attention. She couldn't hear anything. Glancing out the window, it appeared that the rain had let up, although the sky still looked gray and gloomy.

"Max, what is it?"

The dog ignored her, still focused on some noise at the back of the house. Finally, Abby got to her feet, and started to head toward the kitchen. Max scrambled to her feet and followed Abby, then suddenly barked and ran ahead, through the kitchen and to the back door. Startled, Abby followed Max, wondering what was wandering around outside on this wet evening.

Just as Abby was almost to the door, a knock made her jump, and Max barked even more aggressively. Abby hesitated for a moment, looking at the dog. She'd heard a lot of sounds come out of the animal, but never had she heard such a normal, dog-like reaction to anything in the last week, and it unnerved her. In her mind Max had taken on an almost supernatural aura, and to see her act like a common dog protecting her house was disturbing.

The knock sounded again, and Abby told herself to stop being foolish. Resisting the urge to peek through the curtain shielding the window, Abby turned the handle, and opened the door to find Gracie Thomas standing on the back porch, arms crossed, and face twisted in an expression of impatience which she quickly suppressed.

"Uh, hi Gracie. I'm sorry it took me a while to get to the door." Max had stopped barking, but she stood close behind Abby, hackles raised, giving Gracie what Abby considered to be the canine version of the "stink eye."

"Good evening, Abby. I'm sorry to come unannounced. I drove over to see Adam, since he was so upset when I talked with him last night..." The older woman gave Abby an accusing look. "He and Jenn are out for the evening, but I thought instead of wasting the trip, maybe we could talk?" The slightly ditzy older woman of the other night was gone, and in her place a determined mother bear. Abby figured she'd have some explaining to do, even if Adam had tried to smooth things over.

"Yes, certainly. Please come on in." Abby stood back to allow Gracie to enter, bumping into Max in the process. "Max, back up, let Gracie in."

Max backed up, but continued to stare at Gracie with an unnerving intensity. Gracie looked at her for a moment, and then laughed nervously.

"She sure doesn't care for me, does she? Even back when your uncle was alive she didn't like me too much. I always figured it was because she knew I was the *other* woman in Gordon's life." Gracie gave Abby a conspiratorial wink which made her feel uncomfortable. From what Adam had said, her uncle never had any interest in Gracie, but instead put up with her for Adam's sake.

Was Gracie really so clueless and desperate that she

failed to realize Gordon hadn't cared for her, and had instead deluded herself into believing he'd truly had romantic feelings for her?

Instead of following that potentially awkward line of thought, Abby decided to get right to the point. "Not that I'm not happy to see you Gracie, but what can I do for you?"

"I called Adam last night to see how he was doing, and he mentioned to me that you'd accused him of killing Gordon. I thought that must be a mistake, but he was pretty adamant about the whole thing, so I thought maybe we should talk."

Abby was taken aback at Gracie's comment. From what Jenn had said that morning, while Adam had discussed the situation with his mother, it didn't sound like he'd told her that Abby had actually accused him. Suspected him maybe, but not accused.

"I'm sorry, Gracie. There was a huge misunderstanding. I saw something in Adam's shop, a dark green flannel rag, and wondered where it came from since it looked like a torn sleeve that Max found here when I first arrived. I wondered if it could have had anything to do with Gordon's death, since Max was so fixated on it." Abby gestured toward the counter where the sleeve and the single filthy glove sat. Something crossed her mind, eluding her for a moment. Then she remembered she'd left the other glove in the shed and made a mental note to go get it in the morning. It would be safe enough where it was for now.

"I never believed that Adam could have done anything to hurt Gordon. I know how much he cared for my uncle, and how much my uncle cared for Adam."

"You're right, Abby." Gracie nodded with complete understanding, a gentle smile on her face. "Gordon looked on Adam as a son. Really, you know, Adam should have been the one to inherit the farm."

"Uh..." Abby looked at Gracie, momentarily at a loss for words. She felt like someone had just lobbed a mortar round into the room. It wasn't that Abby hadn't felt the same thing numerous times, but she was completely unprepared for Gracie to put it into words so bluntly. Even Max, standing at Abby's side, was silent.

"Still, I'm glad that you've come to your senses about that whole thing. Umm, I smell the wood stove going. Maybe we could go into the living room and sit and chat for a little about your investigations?"

Urgh! The last thing Abby wanted to do was sit and have a conversation with Gracie. Still, she didn't want to insult Adam's mother so soon after their own misunderstanding. She valued Adam and Jenn's friendship too much.

"I guess so, Gracie. Can I get you anything to drink?"

"Oh don't worry about it, Abby. Thank you for the offer though."

As Gracie started for the living area, she picked the green flannel rag and the leather glove off the counter.

"You know, you really shouldn't keep anything like this sitting around in the house. They could have bugs and mold. It's not very healthy. Strange you only have one glove." At Gracie's action, Max started to growl slightly, and move forward.

"Max, no. Really, it's fine Gracie, I..."

Before Abby could get out another word, Gracie opened the door of the wood stove and threw the items on the flames.

"No!" Abby rushed forward, grabbed the tongs from the stand at the side of the stove and pulled the rag out of the fire. She dropped it on the brick where she stamped on the material, trying to put out the flames, at the same time looking for the glove in the growing blaze fed by the increased oxygen from the open door.

In the next few seconds so many things happened at

once, that afterward Abby could never sort out what occurred first. A sudden sharp pain in her head drove Abby to the ground, narrowly missing striking her forehead on the edge of the wood stove. She remembered looking up groggily, and seeing Gracie standing there with the poker from the fire set in her hands. Abby's thick ponytail had cushioned her head from some of the force of the blow, but not enough. A look of profound sympathy was on Gracie's face that was almost more terrifying than anger would have been.

Max erupted in fury, and launched herself toward the woman. Gracie swung the poker almost casually striking the dog over the head, knocking her to the ground where she lay apparently lifeless next to Abby.

The fire popped and a few sparks flew out of the still open door. Gracie reached over Abby's body, closed and latched the door.

"You know, burning the house down could have its advantages, but Adam is going to need it when he inherits the farm."

Abby shook her head, sure she was hearing things. Unfortunately, shaking her head increased the pain greatly, and she groaned. Forcing herself to focus, she pushed herself to her knees and sat back on her heels so she could see Gracie where she stood, still holding the poker.

"What do you mean? I don't understand." Abby felt like she was going to be sick.

"That's easy. Your will names Adam as your heir."

Abby was sure that the blow to her head had scrambled her brain, and she was no longer able to understand English.

"I don't have a will. I haven't had a chance to make one."

"Don't worry, dear. I decided to help you out since I was sure you didn't have time. It will be found among your other paperwork, naming Adam the sole beneficiary. When it comes down to it, I would have preferred he marry you, and get the farm that way, but it appears that he's determined to keep that barren girlfriend of his. Besides, you refuse to give up looking for what happened to your uncle, and we can't have you doing that. Now come on, get up. We're going down to the lake."

Abby looked blearily up at Gracie, then started to push herself to her feet. Max was twitching, and Abby felt a surge of relief that the dog was still alive. The next instant that relief was squashed as Gracie jabbed at Abby with the poker. She staggered and thought she would fall again only catching her balance at the last moment.

"It wasn't an accident you came when Adam wasn't home was it? You knew he'd be out."

"That's right, though I thought it would sound better to you if you thought I'd just missed him. You might be suspicious if you knew I'd come here just to see you. You might not have let me in."

Abby watched as Gracie quickly picked up the piece of cloth Abby had rescued from the fire, opened the stove door and deposited it back inside. Abby watched as it burst into flame. Already there was no sign of the single glove, and the flannel was quickly consumed. This time there would be no saving them.

There's still the glove in the boat shed. I still have that. Abby held on to that thought. Maybe between that glove and the paddle they would have the evidence they needed to prove what happened.

"I believe there was something else? I talked to Adam this afternoon, and he mentioned something about a paddle? He sounded pretty excited about it. Apparently he thinks that it can help pinpoint your uncle's killer."

Abby remained silent, but her heart sank. Jenn must have told Adam about her find, and he'd passed it along, not realizing what he was doing. Abby had already lost the sleeve and the glove. The paddle was her best chance.

She couldn't let it go because without it she wouldn't...

Suddenly her mind slammed into gear. It probably didn't matter about the sleeve or the glove, and maybe not even the paddle. It was obvious that Gracie had either killed her uncle, or was protecting someone else. She was unhinged. All Abby had to do was...

All Abby had to do was survive, and that wasn't looking like a really good prospect at the moment.

"Where's the paddle, Abby?" Grace demanded. She lifted the poker as if to swing it again.

Well, if the paddle made a weapon once, it can be one again. Abby started to walk toward the broom closet just inside the kitchen.

"Gracie, I don't understand." She tried to keep her tone as placating as possible. "You said you were glad that I was looking into my uncle's death. I thought you were happy that I didn't think he'd just had an accident."

"It made Adam happy to think that Gordon hadn't just gotten drunk and fell into the lake. He took your uncle's death pretty hard, and the idea that he didn't do it to himself seemed to give him some form of hope." Gracie had a far away, sad look in her pale blue eyes.

"You know, I didn't intend it to happen the way it did... didn't honestly intend for it to happen at all. But it did, and now I have to make the best of a bad situation." Gracie spoke almost conversationally, as though they were discussing what to make for dinner, not the death of another human.

Seeing Gracie momentarily distracted, Abby grabbed for the handle on the broom closet and ripped it open, reaching for the paddle. Her hand slid around the shaft, and Abby turned to swing at Gracie only to see her close behind, swinging the poker.

The metal implement met the wood of the paddle before Abby's swing picked up any type of speed. The resulting impact knocked the paddle from Abby's hand

and it clattered to the ground, sliding across the floor out of Abby's reach.

Gracie lifted the poker again, and prepared to take another swipe at Abby who raised her left arm to protect her head. The blow came, causing her arm to go numb from elbow to finger tips, and Abby wondered briefly if it was broken. The pain drove her back to her knees where she cradled the arm, and waited for the final blow.

It didn't come.

"Abby, I really don't want to have to drag your body down to the lake, but I'm not going to have you keep trying to get away." Still Gracie maintained that calm, almost gentle tone which chilled Abby to the bottom of her soul.

Keeping eyes on Abby, Gracie backed over to the counter, and pulled out the drawer that Abby had come to think of the "junk drawer" and pulled it open. Glancing inside, she pulled out a roll of silvery duct tape.

"This should do it," Gracie said cheerfully. "Now here," she extended the roll out to Abby, keeping the poker in her other hand at the ready. "Wrap this around your left wrist."

Abby debated her options. Her left arm was still useless, but Gracie only had one hand on the poker. She wouldn't be able to swing it with as much strength, and maybe, just maybe, Abby would be able to wrestle it away from her.

It was almost as if Gracie could read her mind. The older woman set the roll of duct tape down on the kitchen table and backed up and gestured for Abby to pick up the roll.

"Now, wrap the tape around your left wrist, then put your hands behind your back." Gracie put both hands back on the poker and Abby knew that if she were to rush the older woman, she wouldn't stand a chance.

Abby took the roll of tape and wrapped it twice around her left wrist, wincing at the pain. Then, looking at Gracie, she turned and held her arms behind her back, the roll of tape dangling from the useless left wrist.

She could sense Gracie approach, and felt the woman grab her right wrist and yank it across behind her back, making Abby's shoulder twist in pain. She couldn't see behind her, but she could feel both of her wrists taped together, effectively immobilizing her. She tried to pull her hands apart with no success. Just additional pain in her injured left arm.

Gracie backed away from Abby, the feeling of warmth from her proximity turning cold. Abby turned to see Gracie, poker still in one hand, bend to pick up the paddle from where it had landed on the other side of the kitchen.

"Okay Abby. Let's go down to the lake." Gracie gestured for Abby to walk over to the back door where she stood, unsure what to do next.

"I can't open the door with my hands behind my back like this."

"Fine." Gracie sounded annoyed. "Stand back out of the way.

Abby did as she was commanded, and with both the paddle and the poker in one hand, Gracie reached over and pulled the kitchen door open, then stood back and prodded Abby to go through. Abby stumbled on the rim of the door jamb and nearly fell, catching her footing at the last moment.

"Move it. I haven't got all night. Adam and Jenn usually get back fairly early from these types of activities, and I really don't want them to know I was here."

"What are you going to do?" Abby asked, pretty sure that she already knew the answer, and wasn't going to like it.

"I figure if you're so interested in how your uncle died, that maybe I'd show you. I'd hate for you to die unsatisfied."

Gracie pulled the door shut, and the two headed around the house and down the trail toward the dock.

Abby stumbled several times in the dim light, her balance impaired by her hands' awkward position. Each time Gracie prodded her with the paddle and urged her on, sounding less gentle now, and more irritated by Abby's clumsiness.

As Abby approached the dock she heard a noise back up at the house. Max had apparently regained consciousness and was barking and howling. She could hear banging on the window in the front of the building, but it appeared that Gordon had invested in some pretty strong tempered glass as she didn't hear any shattering.

When they got to the edge of the dock, Abby hesitated. It was a long dock, nearly fifty feet, and the far end protruded over the start of a deep drop off. With her hands tied behind her back, Abby would have no chance of swimming if Gracie intended on knocking her into the water. Abby debated on whether she could head butt Gracie, and knock her in the water instead. It wasn't a good option. The odds were good that they'd both go in, and ultimately, if Gracie wasn't injured, she'd still be able to drive Abby under the water. Still, it was the only option she had. If she didn't go into the water, she could potentially run off the dock and hide in the rapidly dimming light.

Gracie poked her in the back, insistent on Abby to keep moving.

They were almost halfway to the end of the dock when Gracie started talking again, in a sort of dreamy singsong voice that chilled Abby to the bones.

"Like I said, I didn't come here that night intending to kill your uncle."

Abby started to turn around, expecting at any moment for the paddle or the poker to come out of nowhere and knock her into the water where she'd sink like a stone. No blow came. Gracie was standing a few feet away, looking around the lake. The expression on her face matched the dreamy tone of her voice.

"It could have been so much easier. I thought if he and I got married then Adam could inherit naturally as my child. After all, Gordon already treated him like a son. But when I suggested it to Gordon, he laughed at me. He said he wasn't going to marry anyone."

Abby could hear hurt in the woman's voice and watched her face twist in remembered pain.

"I cared for him, I actually did, and he should have married me."

"I'm so sorry if my uncle hurt your feelings, Gracie. I can see how much you cared for him, and it had to have hurt terribly."

"It did hurt. I told him that even if he didn't want to marry me, that he should leave the farm to Adam. Gordon didn't have much time, what with the cancer and all, but he wouldn't hear of it. Said that you were his niece, and the last of his family. He was so sure that you'd want to stay. I guess he was right, huh?"

"But why kill him, Gracie? If he only had a little time left, why take that away from him?" Abby's pain showed in her voice.

"Because of what he'd tell Adam about me. I didn't want Adam to know. I couldn't bear that. Adam had said he was embarrassed of how I was 'chasing' your uncle. I didn't want him to know that your uncle rejected me. I knew then what had to be done." A chilling smile crossed Gracie's face.

"Where was Max during all this? Certainly she wouldn't let you hurt my uncle without doing something." *Keep her talking, keep her talking...* Abby searched for more questions, comments, anything that would delay Gracie's final action.

A crafty smile appeared on Gracie's face. "Oh, I was prepared for Max. When I got there, I headed up to the fish house. I figured she'd come up to see what I was doing there. When Max reached the shed, I already had the door unlocked and was inside. She came in... she knows me, you see, so she barked a couple of times, then stopped. I ran out the door, and slammed it shut with her inside. She was able to get one of my gloves off my hand, but otherwise it was easy."

Ah, so that was where the glove came from. No wonder she wanted them destroyed. Maybe there was DNA on the inside of them.

"So, you were planning on killing my uncle all along?"

"No," Gracie said patiently, as if talking to a slow learner. "It's just that Max never liked me much, and when she was around Gordon always paid more attention to her than to me. I was hoping she'd be outside when I got there, since Gordon always liked to sit out on the deck at night. If she wasn't, well I was prepared to cross that bridge when I came to it."

"How did you get in the fish house? It's kept locked." They were approaching the end of the dock, and Abby knew that there wasn't much time left to make her own move.

"That part was easy. I know where Adam keeps his keys, and I knew that he and Jenn were going to be out that evening. He'd mentioned he was taking her into town to see a new movie, and they were probably going to get home late. I've got a key to his house, and I just let myself in, borrowed his keys, and on the way home I put them back. They always take Jenn's Jeep when they go into town, so I was sure his keys would be there."

Abby glanced behind her. She was almost out of time, she could feel it. Pretty soon Gracie would get tired of talking, and then she'd act. If Abby was going to rush her, she needed to do it soon.

"Um, so, you were on the deck talking. How did he get in the water?" Abby could hear the growing strain in her voice, but Gracie didn't seem to notice. She still had that same strangely dreamy tone to her voice and distant look in her eye. Abby started to turn, but Gracie's look immediately sharpened and she lifted the paddle higher again, ready to swing.

Abby froze, and in a moment she saw Gracie begin to relax and that dreamy, unfocused look settled in her pale eyes again.

"The loons were out that night, calling, and the full moon was so beautiful, I asked if we could walk down to the shore. He agreed. After all, who would be afraid of someone like me. He was out on the dock. The paddles for the canoe were sitting there, so I picked one up and hit him with it."

Gracie talked matter-of-factly, as though it were something done every day.

"He started to fall and grabbed my arm to catch his balance. I was wearing one of my husband's old flannel shirts, and it tore at the shoulder seems. He tore a perfectly good shirt, so I hit him again.

"He fell into the water dazed, and I pushed him under, down into the muck, with the end of the paddle until he stopped moving. Then I put the paddles into the boat shed and locked the door. No one would ever know that they'd been outside originally." Gracie looked momentarily concerned. "I lost my other glove. I'd shoved it in my back pocket after I locked up Max. When I got home it was gone. Are you sure you haven't seen it?"

Abby fought to keep from looking at the boat shed where the remaining glove was safely ensconced on the shelf. It must have dropped out of Gracie's pocket when she was putting the paddles away after killing Gordon. Max just hadn't been able to get to it earlier because the shed was locked.

"No, I haven't seen any glove other than the one in the house, and I only found that because the dog and the cat were playing with it." Abby mentally crossed her fingers that Gracie would believe her.

"Shame. I don't want to leave any evidence this time. I shouldn't have done it last time, but I thought it would be suspicious if the paddle for the canoe was missing, and I didn't think it would have anything left on it after being down in the water." Gracie grimaced at the thought of her carelessness.

"Is that what you're going to do with me? Knock me into the water and push me under? They're not going to believe that my drowning was an accident, Gracie. Not when I've got my hands tied behind my back. And you know they'll look at Adam and Jenn, if not at you."

"Maybe they won't find you that way. Maybe they won't find you soon at all. These lakes are deep, and the currents are strong in the right places."

Abby had thought that she was already chilled through the bone, that nothing else that Gracie said could cause any more terror, but she was wrong.

Gracie picked up the paddle, and started the last few feet toward the end of the dock and Abby waited for a moment. She didn't want to run too soon, and give Gracie a chance to move aside, or swing the paddle, but too late and Abby wouldn't be able to get up enough speed to knock the older woman aside.

Just as Abby prepared to duck her head and run, she heard a commotion from up the hill by the house. Gracie, distracted from her intention, turned just as Max launched herself from the end of the dock, hurtling into Gracie's chest, and driving her backward. The paddle went flying off into the water, and Gracie stumbled, tried to regain her balance, but continued her backward movement, ramming full force into Abby, and throwing them both off the end of the dock toward the deepest water.

Just before Abby hit the lake with a resounding splash, she heard someone call her name. She started to open her mouth to respond, but there wasn't time.

The water felt like concrete, knocking the wind out of

her. Then the cool water folded over her and drew her down. Abby thrashed her legs, trying to force herself back to the surface. She tried to open her eyes but all she could see were bubbles and swirling murk. There wasn't enough oxygen in her body, and she longed to take a breath, but fought the urge to inhale.

Just as she couldn't stand it any longer she felt an arm grab her from behind. She started to struggle; sure it was Gracie determined to finish the job. She took in a lung full of water, and started coughing.

Moments later her head broke the surface. She choked and coughed, then drew in a breath of cool evening air, and coughed again, still struggling to free herself from the arms holding her captive.

"Abby! Stop! I've got you!" The voice wasn't Gracie's, but male. Her struggles subsided, and she allowed the unseen person to tow her to the dock.

"Can you grab the ladder? I can't lift you up there by myself." The voice asked, close to her ear.

"No." Her voice was harsh with water and coughing. "Hands. Tied."

"Blast. Fine. I'm going to pull you around the side of the dock. Just let me do the work, okay. Don't struggle."

Suddenly a terrified face appeared over the edge of the dock. Jenn.

"Deputy Morrison, is Abby okay?"

That's who had her. Sheriff's Deputy Ben Morrison. Why was he here? Abby tried to turn her head to see him.

"Stop squirming. This is hard enough without you wiggling. The bottom of this lake is like glue." She could hear him breathing hard as he pulled her along the side of the dock.

Abby hadn't even noticed, but she started to feel her feet trailing through the thick muck that made up the bottom of Lake Ellen.

"Where's Gracie?" Morrison asked.

"Adam has her. He's almost got her to shore on the other side of the dock down the beach a little," Jenn answered.

The bottom of the lake started to slope more steeply upward, and Abby could feel stones underneath the mud. She was able to get to her feet, and stood chest deep. A few steps later and the water level was down to her waist, then mid-thigh. Morrison's arm went from actively holding her up, to just providing support.

As soon as she was in shallow enough water, Morrison pulled her to a stop. "Here, let me get that tape off your arms." She stood head down, still breathing hard and coughing periodically. Her wet hair hung down, sticking to her cheek and dripping steadily. She could feel Morrison behind her using something to cut through the tape, pulling at her injured arm and she gasped.

"Sorry. Are you okay? I didn't mean to hurt you." Morrison's voice was full of concern. "Just one more second and..."

Abby felt her arms come free, and pulled her hands in front of her, cradling her injured left arm with her right.

Morrison moved around her, and for the first time she could see he was dressed in jeans and a t-shirt instead of his uniform. Everything was soaking wet, and liberally splattered with muck, and Abby figured she probably looked even worse. The smell of the swamp pervaded every pore. *What a way to impress a guy!*

Morrison didn't seem to notice Abby's disheveled condition, but he had a look of worry on his face as he examined her, taking note of how she was carrying her left arm.

"How badly are you hurt? Someone should be here soon, and we'll get them to call for the ambulance." He took her wrist and began to run his hand up her arm, noticing when she winced and pulled back.

Abby shook her head. "I think I'm okay. Gracie hit me

with a poker, but I think it's more bruised than broken. Maybe cracked. Crap! That hurts!" Ben had palpated the swollen area midway between her elbow and wrist. He gave her the arm back, and she cradled it once again.

"Still, you need to get checked out. Come on; let's get out of this muck." Morrison put his hand under her right arm and helped her move forward, holding her up when the mud threatened to suck her down, and steadying her when she tripped over various roots and branches hidden beneath the soft footing.

As Abby's breathing steadied, she heard a commotion coming from the other side of the dock. She looked in that direction, and in the dim light she could see Adam with his mother in a bear hug, fighting to keep his hold as she struggled against him.

"Where's Max?" Suddenly Abby panicked. Her last sight of the dog had been when she cannoned into Gracie, driving all of them into the water. She'd been hurt. Could she have knocked herself out again in the fall? Was she still in the water?

Abby started to turn and struggle back down to the end of the dock.

"What the...! What are you doing, Abby?" Morrison grabbed her good arm.

"Where's Max? She went into the water when Gracie and I did. She was knocked out earlier. She might be hurt. I've..."

"Max is here, Abby," Jenn said. "On the other side of the dock. She keeps nipping Gracie when she struggles and tries to get away from Adam."

Jenn ducked her head for a moment, her long blonde hair falling forward and shielding her expression, but Abby could have sworn there was a smile on her face. Abby struggled to make the last steps up onto the shore and looked down the bank to where Adam was holding his mother. Max was lying on the ground, head low, eyes intent on the woman. Every time Gracie started to struggle against Adam, Max would slip in quickly and administer a nip on her lower legs causing the woman to yell and kick even more until Max gave her another nip.

Abby bit her lip to keep from laughing. Nothing about this was funny, she thought, but she couldn't help a little burst of giggles from sneaking through. *Must be nerves* she thought.

"Max. Stop that! That'll do!" Adam said breathlessly as the dog swooped in for another nip and Gracie yelped. He looked at Morrison. "Can someone help me here? I'm losing my grip. And someone get Max off us!"

Morrison clambered out of the water and headed for the duo who had wound up at the far edge of the cleared shore. "Abby, call your dog. Maybe she'll come for you."

Yeah, not likely Abby thought, as she clambered from the sand shore up a dirt bank and collapsed on the pine duff, but called out anyway, "Max, come here girl. Leave them alone."

To Abby's surprise, Max's head popped up, and she looked back at Abby, then scrambled to her feet and came running. The dog dropped down immediately in front of her, their eyes meeting.

"Good girl, Max. You're amazing!" Without thinking Abby reached out and scratched the dog's ears, stroking the wet fur on her head, feeling the large lump where she'd been hit.

"Abby!" Jenn was standing looking at them, a huge grin on her face. "She's letting you pet her."

Abby froze and looked at her hand in shock. Sure enough, it was resting on Max's head, and the dog didn't seem to mind at all.

"I guess all I needed to do was to let you save my life, huh?" Abby petted her head, and moved her hand down to dig her fingers in the dog's soggy white ruff. Max leaned into her fingers and groaned in pleasure.

Adam continued to wrestle with his mother as Morrison fished his handcuffs from his belt. With the last click of metal Gracie suddenly slumped in Adam's arms, and started sobbing.

"I just wanted you to be happy, Adam. I wanted you to have the farm," Gracie cried. She was bedraggled, with a smear of muck trailing down her face and milfoil water weed stuck in her hair. Her voice raised in pitch and Max's ears twitched. She growled and Abby was afraid the dog would renew her attack and gripped her collar.

"I wanted you to have a family." Gracie started rocking back and forth against Adam's chest. He kept talking to her in a low voice, trying to calm her.

"No, stay Max. It's okay." The dog glanced back at Abby, and subsided.

The sound of sirens sounded faintly through the evening air, gradually growing closer. Gracie's howls increased in volume with the sirens.

"Mom, it's okay. I know you wanted to help me. You're going to go with the officers." Gracie started to struggle again, and Adam tightened his grip, pinning her arms to her sides.

"Let me have her Adam," Morrison said. "You go up and meet the officers and send them this way. Tell them to call for an ambulance while they're at it."

Morrison reached for Gracie's arm, taking it in a strong grip as Adam let go and stood back. Abby could see tears running down his face, and her heart broke for him. Jenn hurried over and put an arm around his waist and leaned her head on his shoulder. Together, the two of them headed to the top of the hill where Abby could hear them talking to the officers.

Gracie was still crying softly, begging to be forgiven, although Abby couldn't tell if she was begging Adam, God, or Gordon, or maybe even Abby herself.

25

"Gracie still hasn't talked since that night?" Lucy asked.

Abby was relaxing on the couch in the bright front room of the house Saturday evening, cradling her new cordless phone to her ear. Her left arm was firmly encased in a brace and rested on a pillow in her lap. She glanced over at Max, stretched out in the late afternoon sun with Cali Cat by her side.

"Yes, that night by the time the other officers got there, Gracie had broken down. They decided to have her checked out at the hospital, but by the time they got her there, she was just rocking back and forth and staring into space. They've got her in the psychiatric ward right now, and I guess they'll keep monitoring her until she's recovered enough to stand trial."

"She said she killed your uncle, though. Right? So she won't be getting out any time soon." Lucy sounded concerned for Abby's safety. "How is Adam handling all of this?"

"One question at a time! Yes, Gracie told me she killed him, although I'm still not sure if she planned to do it, or if it was a spur of the moment type of thing. I'm not even sure she knows... or knew. We also have the glove that Max found in the boat shed, although that really doesn't prove anything other than she was there with gloves on.

"Gracie also had it in for Jenn. It may just be pure coincidence that she ended up going after Gordon instead of Adam's girlfriend. Of course, Gordon rejected her, and Jenn never did, so that may have been what tipped the scale." Abby sighed. The whole thing was so pointless when it came down to it. Lives changed forever because of this one action on Gordon's part.

"Adam and Jenn have both been great. I was so afraid he'd want to leave because of everything, but they say they want to keep things the way they are. Actually, Adam said that he was afraid I'd want them to leave because of what his mother did to Gordon."

"What made he and Jenn come over that night? That was a piece of luck."

Abby shifted her position, easing her arm which had begun to ache again. Glancing at the loon clock on the wall, she saw it was almost four. Nearly time for afternoon chores. Adam and Jenn were going to come and help her until her arm was better, so she couldn't take too much longer on the phone call.

"Adam and Jenn were at dinner, talking about what had happened with the rag, and my understanding is that Adam said he wished he knew where that particular rag came from as he didn't remember ever having a shirt made of that material. Jenn said maybe it came from his mother, since she'd brought over a bag of rags the week before. I guess it all clicked at that moment and Adam remembered his dad having a chamois shirt like that when he was alive. Adam said he had a terrible feeling something was wrong, and he knew that he'd told his mother I was alone that night, and they'd be in town. So, they left their meal and drove back to Millersburg."

"And that deputy who saved you...?" Lucy let the question trail off.

"What about him?" Abby asked, choking back a laugh. Lucy never changed.

"My question exactly. It sounded like it was a pretty heroic rescue. How did he, Adam and Jenn happen to show up at exactly the right time anyway?"

"Well, part of it was coincidence, I mean them being at the same time. From what Ben told me, he got my message about the paddle, and even though he wasn't supposed to be on duty until the next day, he happened to be out in the area visiting friends and decided to stop on his way home. It would save him making the trip out the next day. I mean, we're a little spread out around here and the sheriff's department has a lot of territory to cover.

"He was on his way here, and Adam and Jenn passed him driving like a 'bat out of hell.' He pulled them over, even though he was off duty, and when he got out to talk with them, he recognized who they were. Adam told Morrison his suspicions, and they both put on their 'bat wings' and fortunately got here just in time."

"So what happens now?" Lucy asked.

"Well, for now we just wait and see if Gracie comes out of her daze and can stand trial. And in the immediate sense, I've got to do chores, Luce. Adam should be here any moment to help me out."

"I get it. Kick me off the phone why don't you? Your life is the most exciting thing I've got going on a Saturday afternoon, and you're going to send me off to Saturday night TV, and a bowl of popcorn." Lucy tried to adopt a sulky tone, but Abby could hear the laugh under her voice.

"Well, you're just going to have to come out and visit sometime. We'll get you set up in some muck boots and you can milk the goat. Of course, you'd probably want to consider it before the snow flies from what everyone tells me, unless you've got snow shoes."

"Deal," Lucy laughed as she hung up the phone.

Abby swung her legs off the couch and stood. Max lifted her head at Abby's movement, then rolled onto her chest, dislodging the cat who stood there looking offended.

"Okay, guys, time to do the chores."

Max scrambled to her feet and both animals headed for the back door. As Abby was pulling on her shoes, in preparation for the work ahead, she heard Adam's truck roll down the driveway. Standing, she stubbed her foot on the floor, driving her toes into the shoe. Tying the laces had taken on a whole new challenge with her injured arm, and she'd started just tucking in the ends like the teenagers.

To Abby's surprise, when she opened the door, she saw that Ben Morrison was with Adam and Jenn, and the three of them were walking toward the barn as though they were best of friends.

Max brushed past her and ran out the door and across the barnyard, greeting Adam and Jenn exuberantly. Cali Cat, who had chased the dog across the gravel, seemed to be just as happy to see the humans, but restricted her joy to just rubbing around their legs, nearly tripping Ben at least once.

"Hi Adam, Jenn. Hey Ben, how are you doing?" Abby walked up, smiling at her three friends. "I don't mean to be rude or anything, but if you're here, Deputy Morrison, you're going to be put to work."

"Hey Abby, I'm not afraid of a little work." Ben smiled at her. "I was just going by Adam's, and I thought I'd stop and see how all of you were doing. Adam and Jenn were on their way up here, so I came along for the ride."

The last time Abby saw Ben was Thursday morning following the rescue the night before. She, Adam and Jenn had all gone to the station to give their statements concerning Gracie's attack on Abby Wednesday evening.

Abby found that while the assault was terrible, so much was happening at once, she only had time to react. This long, drawn-out dissection of Gracie's mental breakdown was almost more painful. Her heart ached for

Adam, and she felt profound gratitude for Ben's presence throughout the ordeal.

Abby smiled at her three friends. "Well, Ben, I guess we need to check you out. How are you at milking a goat?" She waved her left arm in the air. "This thing means I get to put of milking duties for a few more weeks."

"And that you get to avoid carrying buckets of fish pellets up the hill," Adam added laughing.

"Well, you wouldn't want me to be off balance by carrying just one bucket, would you?" Abby said, a look of mock indignation on her face.

"The doctor said it was just a cracked ulna, right?" Adam asked. "That shouldn't take too long to heal."

Abby nodded. "Yes, she said I was lucky that a blow like that didn't break both bones, but just the ulna. There's a lot of bruising, but she said it should be pretty well healed in a few weeks. I don't even have to wear the brace all the time, and I was able to type on the computer without too much pain this morning." Abby saw Adam start to open his mouth and she knew what was coming.

"Don't get any ideas, Adam! I'm not ready to milk the goat."

Jenn started to laugh and Ben and Adam joined her. Abby herself laughed, happy to see that the dark clouds of the past week were starting to dispel.

It didn't take four people long to finish the chores. Jenn stayed down in the barn, tossing hay to the pasture animals, and milking Autumn. Abby gladly let the two men carry the buckets of food up the hill for the fish, while she contented herself with less strenuous chores, such as tossing a few handfuls of pellets out into the pond so that she could see the trout swarm around in a feeding frenzy. It was like having a gigantic aquarium or koi pond, and she found she enjoyed coming out on the hill even when it wasn't feeding time, just to watch the fish.

Abby was studying the pond of juveniles and occasionally throwing out a few pellets when she felt someone walk up behind her. She turned, and saw Ben, watching her watch the fish.

"Pretty cool, huh?" Abby asked smiling at him.

"Yep, pretty cool... and soon to be pretty tasty." He grinned at her expression. "I take it you've decided to stay, Ms. Williams?"

"Yes, Deputy Morrison. I've decided to stay. Of course, the first winter may make me change my mind if everything they tell me is true. I'm not used to living in a place where I can't drive for an hour and be out of the snow."

"You're tough, you'll get used to it."

"Uh huh." Abby could hear a slight note of skepticism in her voice, and squashed it down. "Where's Adam?"

"He headed back down to the barn to check on Jenn. See if she needed any help. All the chores up here are done, but you were so involved in your communion with your fishy friends here, that you didn't hear him call."

"Yeah, get over it," Abby grumbled good naturedly. "Come on, then. I've got some things to talk to the two of them about."

Abby and Ben made their way down the hill and into the barn.

"Adam?" Abby called out, peering around the dim space. "Are you in here?"

"I think he's up in the loft, moving some hay." Jenn's voice floated out of the side room where she was milking Autumn.

Abby paused, holding her breath, and she could hear the sounds of something heavy being shifted around from above.

"Hey Adam, can you and Jenn come to the house for a minute after we're done here?"

Adam's head appeared over the edge of the loft. "I'll

be right down, Abby. I think Jenn is about done. What's going on?"

"There's just something I want to talk to you about."

A few minutes later the four walked to the house, accompanied by the dog and cat.

"I hope there's nothing wrong." Adam looked over at Abby, concern on his face. "You have decided to stay, right? You haven't changed your mind?"

"No, I haven't changed my mind." Abby smiled at Adam and Jenn to reassure the couple, then ushered them all into the kitchen. "I just felt that there were a few things that needed to be addressed. Go ahead and have a seat. Can I get anyone something to drink?"

"Come on, Abby," Jenn laughed. "We're dying here! What's going on?"

Abby grinned at the three. "Fine, I'll put you out of your misery." Abby went to the counter and picked up a manila folder, then turned back to the group at the table. "Adam, I know how much my uncle meant to you, and you to him. It's bothered me that he left everything to me, and I think if things had been different, he would have made some changes to the trust."

Adam looked up at Abby, emotions warring on his face. Jenn reached out and took his hand and gave it a squeeze, and Abby saw her give him a reassuring look.

"I know the trust was dissolved when my uncle died, but I figured I could make one final, executive decision as trustee." Abby handed the folder to Adam who took it with shaking hands and opened the cover. "It's the deed, to your house and shop, as well as five acres around it. Minus my driveway, of course."

Adam and Jenn looked at the papers in silence, then up at Abby, and she could see unshed tears in his eyes.

"I..." Adam's voice was thick, and he cleared his throat. "I don't know what to say, Abby. Especially after what my Mom did. I can't thank you enough." Adam pushed his chair back, stood and gave Abby a bone crushing hug!

"It's what Gordon would have wanted, huh Max?" Abby looked down at the dog at her side. Max answered with a soft woof, and her puff-ball tail twitched back and forth.

"So, can I interest anyone in some cherry beer? I found Gordon's stash."

The others laughed at her comment, and Abby headed to the refrigerator where she'd put the bottles to cool earlier in the day. Suddenly Max barked, startling the four friends. A knock on the door announced another visitor to the farm.

Abby looked back over her shoulder as she walked to the door. "Hey Jenn, the beer is on the top shelf. Do you mind?"

She turned back to the door just as another knock sounded even louder. She frowned slightly. Who was being so impatient?

"I'm here, for pete's sake," she muttered under her breath. Turning the knob, she pulled the door open to see the new visitor.

"Josh!" Abby couldn't have been more surprised if a alien spaceship was parked in the barnyard.

"Hi Abby. Can I come in?"